CHAKWA: THE LABYRINTH

KSHAMA AGHAMKAR

Contents

Preface   *v*

Acknowledgements   *vii*

1. SEASONS CHANGE   1

2. SOMETHING LURKING?   5

3. REMINISCE   10

4. KNOCK KNOCK   13

5. GATECRASH   20

6. FRESHLY BREWED TEA ?   28

7. FOLIAGE AND WELL, IF IT WORKS   31

8. UNDERCURRENTS   38

9. LAKESIDE VIEW   52

10. RUMOUR HAS IT...   55

11. THE SOUND OF TROUBLE   59

12. DIGGING THE GRAVE   62

13. LOST AND FOUND?   65

14. THREADS THAT BIND   69

15. THE LEGEND OF CHAKWA   73

16. MAYDAY MAYDAY   79

17. CIRCLES... ON LOOP   86

Preface

Feeling the thrill of the unknown and the comfort of a tale well-told, I welcome you to the mystical realm of Chakwa, a labyrinth of secrets, ancient mysteries, and forgotten lore. As Abhay and Kavya embark on this journey together, the boundaries between reality and myth blur, and the whispers of the past grow louder.

Inspired by the intricacies of the human experience, "Chakwa: The Labyrinth" is a testament to the tale of adventure, self-discovery and the unrelenting human spirit.

Acknowledgements

I am forever grateful to the individuals who have supported me on this incredible journey. To my mother, Vidya Aghamkar, for being my rock, my guiding light. For her belief in me has been the driving force behind my writing.

To my friend Elton Perpetuo Paixao Fernandes, I offer sincere thanks for your exceptional creative talent and expertise. Thank you for your consultation throughout the publishing process.

With heartfelt appreciation and love,
Kshama Aghamkar

CHAPTER ONE

SEASONS CHANGE

(Glitches in the car stereo)
Runaway but we're running in circles
Runaway, runaway ...
Raindrops slowly sliding onto the glass, covering the car window, making Abhay and Kavya contemplate about what to do next.
(Circles- Post Malone, continuing in the background)
I dare you to do something,
I'm waiting on you again.
So I don't take the blame.
Runaway but we're running in circles
Runaway, runaw--
The song stops suddenly. Abhay scratches his beard for a moment and proceeded to grab something from the air vent compartment. He was noticeably restless. Taking the vent off without breaking it, he held an older version of the Nokia cell phone. Pressing the keys, he was trying to access the contact list. The keyboard sound was loud enough to make the Green Bee- Eater birds around stop their chirping.

Abhay stepped out of the car to receive a proper signal.

" Yeah. Hi. I've done it. Hmm... Hmm..."

Kavya unbuckled her seatbelt and leaned next to Abhay's seat, as she strained to catch every word, while Abhay was leaning on the car.

"I did exactly the way you asked me to. Yeah, she's here with me..." Abhay paused for a few seconds. " Hmm. All alone, nobody around.."

As he spoke in hushed tones, Abhay's eyes flicked towards Kavya as he sensed her proximity. Kavya quickly tried to grab her bag, tried to unlock the door but Abhay gestured he has locked it. He then got inside.

"Why did you actually bring me here, Abhay? Who were you talking to? It didn't sound like you were calling someone for help...", Kavya asked with a panicked tone.

"It wasn't me. I swear the road brought us here. You have to believe me." He justified.

"I didn't know you had a spare phone hidden inside the car. You never told me about it."

"I'm the one keeping secrets now, Kavya? Honey, what about the pepper spray and the utility knife you carry in your bag?"

Kavya was dumbstruck.

The weather was ideal for a for a romantic getaway. The monsoon rain had transformed the landscape, infusing the air with a refreshing coolness. Leaves rustled softly, the trees swayed in gentle harmony. But inside the car, tension simmered between Abhay and Kavya contrasting the welcoming atmosphere outside. After sometime, dark clouds gathered once more, shrouding the forest in an ominous veil. The forest's eerie silence enveloped the car,amplifying Kavya's anxious breaths. Her chest tightened with every passing moment. Abhay noticed her distress and grabbed a water bottle from the backset. Kavya refused the offering, her eyes narrowing. Abhay's nostrils flared as he closed the bottle cap. His jaw clenched, he gazed out the window. Kavya craved fresh air, but as she reached for the window, Abhay's voice cut through the silence.

'Don't open the window. Keep it shut." His tone dripped with a warning.

Kavya's gaze drifted from the serene view to Abhay's profile, her mind racing with doubts. Why did he insist on keeping the windows shut? His tone hadn't indicated concern; it was firm, almost commanding. She fidgeted with her seatbelt, her unease growing.

" Abhay you know I'm claustrophobic. We've been trapped in this car for hours. I'm beginning to feel dizzy. Kavya talked, her breaths growing shallower. "That Misal Pav from the stall wasn't a good idea. My stomach's churning." Abhay's eyes locked onto the path ahead, his grip tightening. The narrow trail, overgrown with twigs and vines, disappeared into the haze. Tall Banyan trees loomed with their canopies filtering the fading sunlight above. The air was heavy with damp earth and decaying leaves. "We need to get out of here before dark." Abhay said, his tone laced with urgency. Kavya sensed his panic, realizing he hadn't planned to bring her here. But was it somewhere else instead? Abhay's expression remained cryptic. "I think we should go for it." Abhay continued, his voice firmer. "This path has to lead somewhere. We have no other option." The trees seemed to close in round them, casting longer, darker shadows. Abhay's knuckles whitened on the wheel, his eyes fixed on the path ahead.

Kavya pondered if Abhay's stare was linked to the recent disagreement between them. The unspoken tension between them had grown over the past two months, a slow burning fire that neither dared to acknowledge. Abhay avoided confrontation, while Kavya hesitated to broach the subject. She was excited when Abhay suggested to visit Khandi Point for the weekend. Kavya wondered if this trip would finally ease the unspoken tension between them. It would also be a distraction from their mundane lives, she thought.

They'd always cherished their road trips, bonding over music and laughter. Earlier today, Abhay broke the ice, handing Kavya the AUX cable. As they jammed to ' Tumhe baarish bada yaad karti hai' and 'Afreen, Afreen', Abhay's eyes sparkled. He chimed his keychain and pecked Kavya's cheek. Kavya reciprocated, her heart fluttering. She savoured the moment, reminiscent of their courtship days. Kavya felt a pang of nostalgia, longing for the carefree days when love was new.

As they meandered through the narrow trail, the golden hue of Sonki flowers, coupled with the lavender blush of the rare Karvi shrubs blanketed the trail. Butterflies danced amidst the blooms, oblivious to the monsoon rain lurking behind. The atmosphere was surreal, like a Disney movie landscape.

CHAPTER TWO

SOMETHING LURKING?

Abhay's warm breath caressed Kavya's ear, whispering something. Their lips almost touched when Kavya's gaze drifted, sensing an unsettling presence. She narrowed her eyes, her focus drawn to the shrubs. "What's wrong?', asked Abhay, following her gaze. "You see someone?" "No. I feel like we're being watched." Kavya said. Abhay chuckled. "Must be a snake or something." Kavya raised an eyebrow. "You're quite romantic today." Abhay's smile faltered as he stared out Kavya's window. "Shh.. Just enjoy this moment."

A brown hare darted across the shrubs, its agile hind legs propelling in a zigzag pattern. They watched in awe. "Hey, your friend!", Kavya teased, nudging Abhay. As they observed the hare and its companions grazing, Kavya''s unease lingered, a nagging sense that they weren't alone.

Was something lurking around? Suddenly, everything came to a standstill. The wind blew in Kavya and Abhay's direction, carrying the sweet scent of flowers, as if someone had freshly applied perfume after a shower. Just then, the birds stopped chirping, twigs began snapping. "Perhaps there's a predator around." Abhay guessed. "I read that this area encounters a couple of leopards every few days."

"Do we stop the car engine and wait for some time?", Kavya asked.

"I think so," Abhay replied "I'll drive next to those shrubs there. We can wait for a bit."

"Yeah, sounds good."

They proceeded to wait near the shrubs. After noticing nothing suspicious for quite some time, they decided to move forward when they were interrupted by a loud "meow" squawk. The call was loud, like a signal. Then a magnificent peacock appeared, spreading its majestic, colourful wings. Kavya quickly took out her phone, scooting and positioning herself to capture a picture-perfect shot of this elusive yet beautiful bird.

"Ah. The camera doesn't do justice to its beauty. Look!" She showed Abhay her phone. Abhay gestured for her to take more pictures. "I wish I could go out and take a few more."

"Be careful not to scare it away," Abhay cautioned.

Kavya got down and slowly tried getting closer to the peacock for a couple of clicks. Abhay watched her with delight, relishing the moment. She also tried to chase the hares, which later disappeared into shallow depressions in the shrubs.

She returned excitedly showing Abhay the pictures she clicked. "Did you see the side-eye its giving me?" She exclaimed.

"Where?" Abhay looked concerned.

"Well, right in the center, Abhay!"

Abhay took off his shades and narrowed his eyes. "Kavya, I'm unable to see anything. The background is blurry and all I can see are shrubs and the forest. There's no peacock in the picture."

"Seriously, Abhay? I know my photography skills aren't great, and you're trying to pull my leg. Okay, look.. How about... This. This photo? This one?" She scrolled through her gallery, showing him her phone.

"Honey, none of the photos you showed me have a peacock in them."

"Buns. I'm serious now. Okay, do I send these to you to check?"

"I don't know, Kavya... We don't have network here and the connectivity is poor. But it was a lovely sight, wasn't it? I've never seen a peacock in the wild before."

Kavya was busy scrolling through her phone when Abhay stopped her.

"Enough, Honey. We'll click using my phone the next time we spot a peacock, alright?" He consoled.

Kavya didn't know what to make of it. It was as though her sanity was being questioned. This wasn't the first time this had happened.

Kavya was making breakfast one day when the doorbell rang. She wiped her hands and answered it. Varun, Abhay's colleague, stood outside. "Hi Kavya, I'm dropping off some equipment for Abhay's project."

Kavya's curiosity piqued. "Project? I thought Abhay resigned."

Varun hesitated. "Uh, no. We've been working on this new project since a couple of months now."

Kavya's unease grew. She offered Varun tea, but he refused politely, saying he had some other work.

After Varun left, Kavya confronted Abhay as he stepped out of the shower smiling.

"Who was at the door?" Abhay asked.

"It was Varun, dropping of your work equipment." Kavya replied. "You told me you quit, Abhay."

Abhay's expression turned puzzled. "Quit? I didn't say that. I'm just wrapping up some tasks"

Kavya's anger intensified. "That's not what you said. You've taken up a new project, despite telling me you quit. You said we'd start fresh, but it was all lies."

Abhay reassured. "Kavya, don't stress. I'm doing this for us."

"You asked me to turn down the Germany project, saying I deserve better." Kavya countered.

"Exactly," Abhay said. "You deserve better than a temporary gig abroad. Plus, how will you manage things alone?"

"It's not a gig; it's my dream project," Kavya clarified. "And I won't be going alone; Purvi would accompany me. I asked you to join me but you refused."

"Yes, because how could I leave everything for three months?" Abhay reasoned.

Kavya's eyes narrowed. "I want you to call Varun right now and ask him what he meant."

Abhay hesitated but dialed Varun's number.

Abhay: " Hey Varun, Kavya's concerned about the equipment you dropped off. Can you clarify?"

Varun: "Just some USB cables for an Ender 3 Model for our new project."

Abhay: "So, you meant I left the old project, not the organization?"

Varun: "Exactly. You're on a new team, still with us. Why? Is Bhabhi worried about something?"

Abhay: "No. Just wanted to know what's in the bag you got."

Varun: "Oh, alright. So see you at the office soon."

Abhay hung up and turned to Kavya. "See? I told you. I left the old project."

Kavya remained sceptical. "Why didn't you correct me earlier?"

Abhay reassured her, "I didn't want to stress you. I'm doing this for our future. We will move to Bangalore eventually, like we planned."

Abhay's reassurance slightly eased Kavya's doubts.

The argument with Abhay replayed her mind. Amid the forest, the tress' towering presence echoed her inner turmoil. Doubt seeped into her thoughts like the forest's mist.

The peacock picture flashed in her mind. She saw it clearly, but Abhay claimed he didn't. Was she assuming things? Or was he manipulating her? Her mind swirled with questions. Abhay's words lingered but his reassurance soothed her frayed nerves.

CHAPTER THREE

REMINISCE

Kavya's thoughts drifted back to the present. Amidst the forest, she thought, was her love beside her. She pushed away her doubts, focusing on Abhay. Her fingers brushed against his arm. Abhay's gentle gaze met hers. A soft smile spread across his face.

"Hey", he whispered.

"Remember our first meeting?" Kavya asked.

"How could I forget?" Abhay's eyes sparkled.

Kavya and Abhay's families had arranged their meeting. Awkward smiles and laughter filled the initial moments. As they sipped coffee, they delved into each other's lives.

Abhay's endearing smile and nodding encouragement and Kavya's welcoming voice made them feel warm around each other.

A sociologist at the Consulate office, Kavya shared her experience interviewing and accused for her research paper. "I dream of publishing my book one day," she revealed.

Abhay, a design engineer, spoke of his aspiration to create an access- friendly wheelchair.

"I want to make mobility easier for everyone," he said. Kavya admired his noble goals.

Hours passed like minutes as they chatted. Their phones buzzed, parents waiting.

They parted ways, reluctantly. But the connection lingered.

The next day, Abhay messaged Kavya.

"Plans for the weekend?" he asked.

Kavya's heart skipped a beat.

"Mids coming up soon. Assignments due Saturday.", she replied.

"Alright..", he said

Kavya teased, "You planning something?"

"Yes, I was thinking of taking a beautiful lady out for brunch... And later her favourite dessert."

Abhay's response made her blush. "Bold, aren't you?", Kavya playfully asked.

Abhay joked, "Dessert pre- brunch, post - brunch, or breakfast?"

Kavya giggled. "Dessert post- brunch sounds great. No river-crossing early mornings,"

Abhay's soft promise interrupted her. "I don't mind crossing rivers to meet you."

Their Saturday plan was set. "Meet me at 11 near your University?", Abhay confirmed.

At the cafe, Kavya asked, "So, no cucumbers in your sandwiches?"

"This cucumber's raw, not pickled. I'll sprinkle salt and pepper later."

Abhay's explanation delighted her.

"You're in luck; I like raw cucumbers." Kavya said, smiling.

As they chatted, Abhay revealed his interest for pottery.

"I didn't take you for a pottery enthusiast" Kavya said.

"Why's that?", Abhay asked.

"I assumed you were a gamer, into football.."

Abhay chuckled. "Engineers are stereotyped, aren't we?"

"I didn't mean to stereotype. Your DP suggests gaming is your thing.'' Kavya clarified.

"Old picture. I'm barely active on socials." Abhay explained.

"Not active, huh?", Kavya grinned mischievously.

Abhay sensed something. "Anything wrong?", he asked.

"You sent a friend request, deleted it, and stalked someone on LinkedIn?"

Abhay's embarrassment was palpable.

"I thought I was discreet!"

"The receiver gets notified." Kavya informed him.

"God, that was naive!", Abhay chuckled.

"So, Mr. Curious, what did you discover?" Kavya pulled his leg.

"Phone slipped; couldn't stalk you. I can resend the request?" Abhay justified.

"I'll think about it."

Their playful banter filled the autumn morning.

Months passed, their secret meetings continued. Kavya and Abhay stole glances, exchanging sweet nothings. Stolen moments in hidden alleys, whispering promises. Their love blossoming.

CHAPTER FOUR

KNOCK KNOCK

One day, Kavya and Abhay strolled hand-in-hand through the bowling alley, the sounds of laughter and rolling pins filling the air. Their evening had been perfect so far- a strike in bowling, a win in the racing game and shared giggles over cheesy arcade games.

As Kavya triumphantly raised her arms after beating Abhay in the racing game, he spotted a familiar face in the crowd. His heart skipped a beat, but he pushed the thought away. Tonight was about Kavya and he had a surprise planned.

"Hey, let's try the scavenger hunt," Abhay suggested, guiding Kavya toward game area.

"Sounds fun!" Kavya exclaimed.

The scavenger hunt took them through a maze of clues and riddles. Kavya's eyes sparkled as she solved each puzzle. Abhay pretended to help, his heart racing with anticipation. Finally, they reached the last clue.

"It's on the other side of the room," Abhay's voice was casual. "Go grab the box."

Kavya hurried over, her hair bouncing behind her. As she opened the red box, her eyes widened. Kavya's gaze flew to Abhay. He knelt, a rose- shaped container in his hand, a stunning ring embedded in its center.

"Will you marry me?", Abhay asked as he proposed, still kneeling.

Kavya nodded, with tears streaming down her face. "Yes!", she exclaimed.

The staff waited with confetti, ready to celebrate.

"I love you, Abhay, my Bunny Buns!" Kavya whispered.

"I love you too, Honey Hons," Abhay said.

Their love was sealed.

After the proposal, still gushed with the feelings about each other, they walked outside. Kavya excused herself to freshen up. As she stepped out of the washroom, she spotted Abhay hugging a well- built guy in a navy blue hoodie. Her curiosity piqued.

Abhay gestured, "There she is"

The guy turned. Kavya's heart skipped a beat.

It was Daksh, Abhay's school mate and football team companion. Daksh's stare lingered.

Kavya slowed her pace. A semi- smile hid her unease. As Kavya watched Daksh approach, Abhay's grip on her hand tightened. She sensed a mix of warmth and wariness in Abhay's gaze.

"Kavya," Abhay said, "Meet Daksh, my old friend."

No hug from Abhay, just an introduction that sounded formal.

Daksh's handshake was firm. Kavya's unease grew as Daksh's gaze lingered.

"Congratulations," said Daksh. "Join us for a friendly bowling duel?"

Kavya and Abhay exchanged hesitant glances. They reluctantly agreed.

Abhay sensed the unsaid tension between Daksh and Kavya. "Daksh the star football player, always had a way with words... And girls", he thought to himself. The evening's tone shifted.

The lanes were set, the balls polished. Kavya and Abhay v/s Daksh and his friend.

The air thickened with unspoken rivalry. Abhay noticed Daksh's gaze on Kavya as he was getting ready for the duel.

"Let's start," said Daksh, grinning. The game began. Tension simmered.

Kavya's focus wavered, as Daksh's presence unsettled her. "Hey, you okay?" Abhay asked, noticing Kavya's unease. Kavya nodded.

The scores tied. Final frame. It was Daksh's turn. He bowled a strike. Kavya and Abhay needed a miracle. "Come on, Kavya," Abhay urged. Kavya took a deep breath. She bowled, the pins fell. Kavya and Abhay won by hair. Daksh congratulated them. Abhay hesitated while Kavya forced a smile.

"It was fun," Daksh said. Abhay nodded. "We should go," Abhay whispered to Kavya.

"Yeah, it's late," Kavya agreed.

"Will catch up soon," Abhay said as he shook hands with Daksh.

As they prepared to leave, Daksh said, "Abhay, your aim's always been impressive. You've got a good eye." His gaze shifted to Kavya. "And you, Kavya, were always the star. Remember those modeling projects in college? How we would struggle to get the best shot? Helping you with your portfolio..."

Kavya's eyes narrowed. "That was a long time ago." Abhay's interest piqued, he glanced at Kavya.

"Thanks for reminding us, Daksh," Abhay said, his tone light but his grip on Kavya tightening.

Daksh checked his watch. "I should go. Nice running into you both."

As Kavya and Abhay walked to their car, Abhay asked, "You modeled in college?"

"Just a couple of projects. Daksh was into photography and he helped me with my modeling portfolio." Kavya said hesitantly.

Abhay searched her eyes. "Is there something you're hiding?"

Kavya reassured him. "Nothing, Abhay, I promise."

Abhay was still sceptical and asked curiously, "Was there something between you two?"

Kavya's expression turned serious. "Daksh liked me during college but I didn't feel the same way. There was nothing between us."

Abhay's gaze lingered. "Even if there was, I wouldn't judge you. I trust you, Kavya."

Kavya smiled. "Let's focus on tonight. A lovely evening, lovely surprise. Thank you for the most memorable day of my life, Abhay."

Abhay smiled. His stare turned distant. "Good to hear Daksh's love was unrequited. It's his karma."

"Abhay, what do you mean?", Kavya asked, with her brows furrowed.

Abhay's gaze snapped back. "Nothing," he said, "Just forget it."

The car fell silent. Kavya's thoughts swirled. Daksh's words, Abhay's reactions.

Was there a hidden rivalry or was Abhay jealous? She wondered.

Abhay's expression softened. "You're right, we should focus on tonight and our future.."

Kavya smiled. The evening regained its warmth.

Kavya's phone pinged.

" its_dak_g: Daksh Garg wants to follow you," the notification read. Kavya's eyes narrowed. How audacious. She tried to ignore it.

"Is that your mom? Asking where we are?" Abhay's voice broke her thoughts.

" Yes. Checking in, worried as usual." , Kavya lied.

Abhay smiled. "Tell her we'll be home soon."

"its_dak_g: Message Request" Kavya's phone pinged again, her heart skipped a beat.

"Just Mom," Kavya reassured, concealing her unease. Abhay's trusting gaze made her guiltier.

Kavya couldn't shake off the feelings of unease upon reaching home, as she stood before the bathroom mirror, wiping her face with a towel. Her eyes drifted to her phone, where the Instagram notifications awaited. Curiosity got the better of her, and she slipped into bed, phone in hand.

"its_dak_g: I didn't expect to see you again after finals. Honestly, I'd hoped to. Sorry for bringing up your modeling project with Abhay today. It just brought back memories of our time together.. the photoshoots, the fun times.. especially that bridal wear advertisement. I've kept that BTS photo of us as my wallpaper for so long! You, with your eyes squinted and nose scrunched, wearing the charm bracelet I gifted you."

Kavya's nostalgia was fleeting. Seven years had passed; things had changed.

Kavya: "What do you want, Daksh?"

Daksh: "Hey, you're still up? Isn't it late?", Daksh was surprised.

Kavya: "I think you should forget the past and move on, Daksh."

Daksh: "Oh I moved on until I saw you today. The memories kept flooding back. One never truly forgets their first love." His words dripped with longing.

Kavya: "Daksh, that was seven years ago. We were young and naive.", she tried to reason.

Daksh: "My feelings for you were genuine. Please don't trivialize them." He added , "Abhay and his family are conservative. I'm sure Abhay wouldn't mind knowing about your bridal wear project, would he? Us together?"

Kavya: "Why do you care?," she asked, her irritation growing.

Daksh: "Because I care for you, Kavya. You're an independent spirit. Don't you think you should be with someone equally independent?" He justified.

Kavya: "Abhay is independent enough. I owe you no justification. Respect my boundaries." Her anger simmered.

Daksh: " I hope I haven't created a rift between you two..Just worried about you."

Kavya: "I respect you as Abhay's friend. Stop prying," she warned.

Daksh: " I'm sorry. I crossed boundaries. If anything happens, I'll be here for you, waiting... As always."

Kavya: "I'm happy with Abhay." She asserted.

Daksh: "Do you ever think about what could have been?"

Kavya: "No. I don't" she said curtly.

Five minutes passed before Daksh's next message.

Daksh: "Hey, don't worry. Your photos are safe with me.. for now."

She was shocked. Was that a threat? What photos is he talking about? She couldn't respond, her mind racing with memories. She lay awake as she couldn't understand Daksh's cryptic message. The words echoed in her mind, "Your photos are safe with me.. for now." She tossed and turned. What did Daksh mean? "What does he want from me?" Kavya's anxiety intensified. She scrolled through reels, trying to distract herself. Another message from him. 12:09 AM.

Daksh: "Goodnight Kavya, sweet dreams."

Kavya chose to ignore. The silence was unsettling. Kavya decided to meet Abhay at a quiet cafe, away from the prying eyes.

"I need to tell you something." Her voice barely over a whisper.

"What's it?" Abhay's expression turned serious.

Kavya took a deep breath and revealed everything. Daksh's message, the photos, the subtle threats. Abhay listened attentively, his face growing darker.

"Why didn't you tell me earlier?" He asked firmly, but he was gentle.

"I didn't want to make you feel uncomfortable," Kavya felt guilty.

"I understand why you're worried." His voice was calm. "But I want you to stay away from Daksh. Completely."

Kavya nodded, feeling a mix of gratitude and relief.

"I'll handle this. You don't need to worry." Abhay continued.

"Thank you, Buns. Thank you for understanding and making me feel better." Kavya said softly.

CHAPTER FIVE

GATECRASH

Kavya busied herself with last-minute preparations for Abhay's birthday party. The warm glow of of table lamps and floor lamps illuminated the living room, casting a cozy ambiance. Soft jazz played in the background, mingling with the hum of conversation.

The room's minimalist decor, with neutral tones, provided an elegant backdrop for the gathering. The floor-to-ceiling windows, now covered with sheer curtains, allowed glimpses of the city skyline. As Kavya awaited the cake delivery, the doorbell rang. Expecting the delivery agent, she opened the door to find Daksh standing outside, dressed in black. The outdoor lighting cast dramatic shadows on his face.

"Kavya," Daksh said, a hint of a smile.

"What are you doing here?" Kavya's eyes widened in shock.

Daksh held up a gift, a neatly wrapped box in gingham paper, completed with a crisp bow. "I was invited. I brought this along."

Abhay approached, his reflection mirroring in the polished marble floor. "Who's at the door, Kavya?"

Kavya hesitated, then stepped aside, allowing Daksh to enter. Daksh's eyes adjusted to the soft lighting, scanning the room. Daksh greeted Abhay with a hug. Kavya excused herself, walking through the open-plan living area, past the sleek kitchen island, and into the kitchen. Kavya turned to the domestic help, who was arranging pizza canapes on a platter. "Rukmini Ji, can you please ask Abhay to help me with something?" Rukmini nodded and discreetly summoned Abhay.

"Abhay, what's going on?" Kavya whispered.

"Be the bigger person, Kavya," Abhay urged, as he leaned against the kitchen counter.

"This isn't right. Daksh gatecrashed," Kavya accused, her voice low.

"You invited him, remember? Don't be rude."

"I didn't invite him," Kavya's confusion deepened. "He's trying to create a rift between us."

Abhay's eyes locked into hers. "Ensure Daksh enjoys himself, just like our other guests."

Kavya approached Daksh, who leaned against the gallery wall, alone, surrounded by lush, floor-to-ceiling garden plants. The soft greenery enveloped him.

"Who invited you?" Kavya demanded.

Daksh frowned. "Abhay invited me, three days ago. 'Please join for food and drinks this Friday evening.' along with the address." Daksh's eyes locked into Kavya's. "I also received a memo about the dress code - to wear black."

Kavya's unease deepened. Daksh pulled out his phone, scrolling for the message, the screen's glow illuminating his face.

Kavya waited, expressionless.

"I'm unable to find the message... I had it right here.." Daksh muttered, scrolling further.

Kavya's skepticism deepened. "You're lying."

"I'm not. I don't know what happened to the message."

"Daksh, please leave. Now." Kavya's voice turned firm.

Abhay intervened, his voice calm. "Daksh, no, please wait." "Let Daksh stay. His early leaving will raise suspicions."

Kavya interrupted, her tone unyielding. "Please Abhay, listen to me-"

"Kavya, let's not make a scene." Abhay requested.

"You asked me to stay away from Daksh, and now....?" Kavya confronted Abhay, in a whisper.

Abhay, trying to ignore what Kavya said, urged Daksh. "No, please stay, Daksh," his voice warm and inviting. "I'm sorry Kavya had a misunderstanding, and I'm really sorry for the inconvenience."

Kavya's eyes narrowed. Abhay's words spinning this as her misunderstanding. "How can you...?" Her eyes flashed with annoyance.

Abhay's expression turned conciliatory. He gestured to his friends, who were watching the exchange with interest. "Daksh is an old pal," a charming smile spreading across Abhay's face, as he continued, "We've known each other since school. We sometimes get into these... Let's call them 'heated discussions', just like we did after our football matches back in the day."

The group chuckled and the tension in the room began to dissipate.

"Come on, Daksh, let's catch up."

Daksh's gaze lingered on Kavya before he nodded slowly. "Alright, I'll stay for one drink."

The guests proceeded to head to the kitchen island, while Kavya stood near the gallery, her arms crossed. The murmur of conversations and clinking glasses filled the air as Rukmini expertly arranged the snacks and drinks on the kitchen counter.

Abhay leaned against the wall, sensing her annoyance. "Kavya, I didn't mean to call you out like that," "Maybe you invited him by sending the invite to all recipients in your contact list. And it's alright. It can happen."

"Abhay, Daksh said you invited him. Not me. Plus, you said you'd handle Daksh, remember?"

Abhay's expression turned nostalgic. "Yes, and I did handle the situation. Cordially. Because he and I go way back... Well, maybe you sent him an invite using my phone? Like remember the other day, you wanted to use my phone for getting pictures of your niece?"

Kavya shook her head. "I didn't use your phone."

"Anyway, that's not important. Who invited him. Invited or not, we shouldn't ask their guests to leave until they themselves wish to."

Kavya sensed a slight guilt about asking Daksh to leave. Abhay was right. "Fine. You're right." She uncrossed her arms, her shoulders relaxing.

"Let's enjoy the evening." Abhay's smile returned.

"You're right, birthday boy. I just wanted a perfect evening for you, Abhay."

"Hey, it is the best birthday I've had so far," Abhay replied. "Thank you."

Kavya smiled. "I'm glad you liked it."

"A year older, a year wiser," Abhay winked, pulling Kavya close. He wrapped his am around her shoulders, escorting her towards the kitchen island. Kavya's resistance melted away. They joined others, as they shared humourous anecdotes from their school days.

As the evening drew to a close, Daksh approached Kavya and Abhay, his expression sincere. "Thanks for the lovely evening, guys. I really appreciated it."

"Anytime, Daksh. Take care." Abhay smiled, clapping Daksh on the back.

As Abhay turned to greet other guests, Daksh leaned in, his voice low. "Kavya, I wanted to assure you - the photos are still safe with me. I wouldn't share them with Abhay, or anyone else. Given Abhay's past, I think it's best to keep the photos away from his sight."

"What past?" , asked Kavya intrigued.

Daksh glanced around cautiously. "It's complicated, or at least it was. Abhay had... Anger issues.. it was serious.. it's just that I don't want to trigger him. I'm glad you're with Abhay, he seems to be a calmer person now. You seem to have a positive influence over him"

"What do you mean by anger issues?", Kavya's eyes widened.

"At school, Abhay wasn't... calm. He got into fights with someone from another school. It was grave. The police had to intervene and Abhay spent a week in an observation home for battery," narrated Daksh.

"What happened?" She pressed, to know more.

Daksh's gaze flicked to Abhay, who was laughing with friends. "That's the thing... Nobody knows. Abhay never spoke about it. He was almost expelled but his good academic record saved him. Also, a police officer had a word with him and since then he changed. But there were always rumours about Abhay.. you know people whisper.."

"What rumours?" , she demanded.

"It was whispered that Abhay------" Daksh's phone rang, shrill in the silence. Kavya leaned in.

"Sorry I have to take this," Daksh was apologetic. His conversations were hushed but his expressions were grave. He ended the call and turned to Kavya and Abhay. "Sorry, I have to go. Urgent personal matter."

Abhay nodded. "Take care, Daksh."

"Wait, Daksh, what were you---"

Daksh was already gone, leaving Kavya amidst swirling thoughts.

"What were you guys talking about?", Abhay asked as he approached Kavya.

"Nothing much.. Daksh is worried about his sister..and tough time." Kavya fabricated a story.

"I hope everything is okay." Abhay asked, concerned.

Kavya forced a smile. Her thoughts were a mix of concern and determination.

Who invited Daksh if it wasn't Abhay? What rumours was he talking about? Was it regarding his anger issues, the almost expulsion?

After the guests left, Abhay's expression changed. His eyes clouded and his voice trembled. "Kavya, did Daksh say something to you?"

Kavya hesitated, unsure how much to reveal. "What do you mean?"

"About my past.. I know he was hinting at something."

Kavya's heart skipped a beat. "What's bothering you, Abhay?"

"I've never told you.. about what happened in school," Abhay's voice now cracked. "A group of guys from another school... They jumped me and my friend. We were beaten up pretty badly."

"Oh, Abhay, I'm so sorry," Kavya's empathy surged.

"I snapped after that. I started fighting back, but not defending myself... I was looking for trouble. Daksh knows, he was there once."

"But you've changed, Abhay. You're not that person anymore." Kavya's grip on Abhay's hand tightened.

"I swear, Kavya, I'd never hit anyone unprovoked. That was a phase.. I've outgrown it."

Kavya's eyes searched Abhay's face. "What provoked the fight?"

"I don't remember, it's all a blur..." Abhay's expression turned vague.

"You don't remember?"

"No, Kavya. And it doesn't matter. That's my past. I've moved on."

"But your past shapes who you are today. Don't you think I deserve to know?"

"I'm a changed man. That's all that matters."

Was Abhay genuinely trying to leave his past behind, or hiding something?

"Abhay, Daksh seemed concerned -----"

"Daksh is just jealous. He can't accept I've moved on." Abhay's interruption was sharp.

"Okay Abhay," Kavya said slowly. "I'll try to forget your past."

"Thank you, Kavya. That means everything to me." Abhay's relief was palpable.

Kavya stood there, with her mind racing with unanswered questions. She looked at Abhay's phone, which was lying on the couch. No invite sent to Daksh.

Who sent Daksh the invite? Was Daksh lying? How did he know the party details? Kavya's determination solidified. She needed the truth. Recalling Daksh's abrupt departure, Kavya wondered: What was he trying to say?

Despite Abhay's warnings, Kavya decided to text Daksh.

Kavya: "You free tomorrow afternoon?"

Daksh: "Yeah, I am.. around 2 PM. Why?"

Kavya: "Meet me tomorrow at 2 PM, at the tea stall near 5th lane."

Daksh: "Why's that sounding like a smuggling deal, Kavya? Are you alright?"
Kavya: "Yeah I am."
Daksh: "Alright.. But does Abhay know about our meet?"
Kavya: "Yes, he's aware." She lied.
Daksh: "Cool! See ya tomorrow. Bye."

CHAPTER SIX

FRESHLY BREWED TEA ?

The sun cast long shadows on 5th lane's worn pavement, the scent of freshly brewed tea wafting from the nearby stall. Kavya sat on a weathered bench, her eyes fixed on the approaching figure of Daksh.

Daksh arrived. "Smuggling deal, huh?," he teased. His smile faltered as he noticed Kavya's serious expression. "You said Abhay knows about us meeting. I assumed he'd be here too." His eyes narrowed.

Kavya's smile faltered for a moment before she replied, "Yeah, he'll join us in a bit."

"Alright. Let's walk," he suggested.

As they strolled, the sounds of the street filled the silence: vendors calling out, motorcycles humming, and the sweet aroma of street food lingering.

"I need answers, Daksh."

"About what?," he asked, his tone cautious.

"I need the truth about Abhay's past. You said the other day about Abhay's past. There were rumours.."

Daksh stared into oblivion, trying to recollect. "I... I don't remember.."

"You said there was a fight back in school, which almost got Abhay expelled. There were whispers." Kavya's reminder was sharp.

"I said that?" Daksh's eyes widened.

"Don't bluff, Daksh."

"I was drunk. Just blabbering.." Daksh shrugged.

"A drunk man's words are a sober man's thoughts," Kavya countered.

"Man, that was deep," Daksh chuckled. His expression turned nostalgic. "Kavya, I wanted you to have those photos from college because.. I wanted you to remember old times. You were amazing and I thought you had potential in modeling."

Kavya's gaze softened.

"I wanted you to acknowledge," Daksh continued, "that you felt something for me back then."

"Daksh, I did have brief feelings for you, but they were fleeting.. We were young.. I've moved on, now.."

"I know, you're happy with Abhay now. You two are a wonderful couple." Daksh's smile was wistful.

Kavya's eyes locked onto Daksh's. "But I need to know the truth about Abhay's past."

"I agree and I'm so sorry, Kavya," Daksh said, his eyes apologetic. "But I don't remember a thing I said the other day. But I'll ask around, talk to old teammates and let you know, alright?"

"You'll do me a huge favour, Daksh. You have no idea.." Kavya's tension eased slightly, her smile was grateful.

"No favours, Kavya. I want to help. And honestly, hold on to Abhay. He's a great guy and you two are perfect together." Daksh's expression was sincere.

"Thanks, Daksh."

As they parted ways, the sun cast a golden glow over the street.

CHAPTER SEVEN

FOLIAGE AND WELL, IF IT WORKS

Kavya's thoughts were interrupted by the sound of screeching tyres, when the car hit a rock, jolting her awake. "Whoa!!!" Abhay exclaimed, his quick reflexes saving them from a disaster. The car screeched, threatening to careen out of control. Abhay's foot slammed the brakes, but the momentum dagged them forward. Their hearts raced as they skidded across the forest floor.

"Abhay!" Kavya cried out.

The car jerked to a stop, mere inches from a dried piece of land, covered with foliage and dried leaves. The silence was oppressive, punctuated only by the sound of gravel settling.

"That was close," Abhay breathed heavily, relief washing over him.

"Too close," Kavya's expression turned grim.

As they caught their breath, Abhay turned off the engine.

"I'll check the damage," Abhay said, stepping out.

Kavya followed, her eyes scanning their surroundings. The dense forest loomed above, the trees' branches creaking in the wind.

Abhay inspected the car tyres, his eyes scanning the under bush.

"Everything okay?" Kavya asked.

"Checking the tyres," Abhay replied.

Kavya watched as Abhay began to clear away the foliage near the tyre. "What are you inspecting?" Her unease creeping into her voice.

Abhay's expression turned startled. "Come see."

She stepped closer, joining Abhay beside the car, her curiosity overrode her apprehension.

The car's tyre hung precariously over the edge of a well, mere inches from disaster.

"If we'd gone just a little farther..." Abhay's voice trailed off.

Kavya's breath caught. "We would have fallen in."

As they stood together, the foliage parted to reveal a spiral staircase, leading downward into darkness.

"Where does this go?" Kavya whispered.

"I don't know," Abhay's voice was low and he was fascinated.

The silence was broken by the distant sounds of birds, their mournful cries echoing through the forest. Leaves rustled and twigs snapped. The stone walls, once sturdy now withered and worn, seemed to whisper secrets. Vines crawled up the sides, as if trying to claim it.

The well's wooden cover, cracked and rotten, creaked in the wind. A worn wooden bucket, attached to a frayed rope, swayed gently, as if beckoning them closer.

Once, this well might have been the heart of a thriving farm, providing life-giving water. Now, it stood abandoned, a testament to forgotten dreams.

The air reeked of stale water and decay, heavy with the scent of rotten leaves. Kavya's unease grew.

"Abhay, don't," Kavya warned, sensing his intention.

But Abhay's curiosity got the better of him. "I used to draw water from wells like this as child," he said, his eyes gleaming. "My uncle's farm had one. I was always fascinated."

His obsession grew. "I want to see if still works."

"Abhay, this isn't your uncle's farm," Kavya's voice was laced with concern.

"I know, but... It reminds me of those summers." His gaze was fixed on the well, his expression nostalgic.

The wind picked up, whispers seeming to carry on the breeze. The trees cracked, their branches swaying ominously.

"No, Abhay, don't!" Kavya's voice rose.

Abhay's hand closed around the rope, his eyes locked onto the well.

Kavya's grip on his arm tightened. "The water looks stale, and the air... It's not right."

"You're right. Let's check the car and get out of here." Abhay's eyes flashed back to reality, but his fascination lingered.

"Yes please,," Kavya was relieved.

As they turned to leave, the wind carried an eerie whisper, the sound barely audible.

"Wait," Abhay said, his head cocked. "Do you hear that?"

"Hear what?"

"Sounds like... running water."

"That's impossible, Abhay. The well's dry." Kavya's unease spiked.

"Not kidding.. Look!" Abhay exclaimed. "How's it possible? The well's dry.. Where is this clean stream of water flowing from?" He wondered.

"The water looks clean, and we might need it. Our bottles will eventually run out."

Abhay's logic took over. "And it's monsoon season. The lid isn't tight enough, and yet the well is dry?"

"Exactly!" Kavya agreed. "Don't you think it's strange, Abhay? This stream meets here, in this abandoned well..."

"So let's find out where the water is coming from! Can you please grab the bottle from the backseat?"

"Abhay, what if the water's from a nearby factory or something? And is poisoned?"

"Oh God, Kavya, why do you always assumed the worst? The water would be murky in that case, wouldn't it?" Abhay reassured her.

Kavya's doubts lingered. "Yeah, Abhay, but.."

"We have to survive. We need water. We're stranded here, and this could be our only source. We won't be digging far... Just a couple of meters more. I just want to check the source of the water. Only once you see it yourself and are convinced, would you drink it, Kavya?"

Kavya relented. "I guess so... Okay.. Let me grab the bottle."

"Thank you!" Abhay exclaimed, relieved she agreed.

They walked toward the stream, its calm waters reflecting the surroundings. Kavya carefully placed the bottle under the flow, using her scarf as a filter.

The stream's bed gleamed with shiny, pearl- like pebbles, tinted orange- brown.

Kavya's eyes sparkled as she picked one up, playing with it, smiling. "Lovely colour," she whispered.

"Looks pretty in your hand.. What's needed is a band and glue to stick the pebble onto it, making it a beautiful ring. If only we had... Let me look for a twig." Abhay offered.

"It's alright, Buns..," Kavya said, pocketing the pebble. "I'm keeping this with me.. Once we're home, you can make one for me."

Abhay's face lit up, "Sure! I'd love to."

As they filled the bottle, sunlight danced across the stream, illuminating a glint of gold. Abhay's eyes locked onto a shiny wedding ring, partially buried in the pebbles.

"Kavya, look!" Abhay exclaimed.

Her curiosity piqued, she joined Abhay.

"This ring.. it's identical to mine," Abhay said, picking it up.

Memories flooded back. "Remember when I lost my ring before our wedding?" Abhay asked.

Kavya's eyes widened. "No, you never told me!"

Abhay chuckled. "I was embarrassed. We were just two days away from the wedding and I panicked. Luckily, after hours of searching, Ravi found it stuck inside the sofa cushion."

Kavya's surprise turned into amusement. "You never mentioned it during the trial or engagement."

Abhay shrugged. "I might have lost weight. But this ring... It's uncanny."

"What were you doing with the ring anyway? How did it fly?" Kavya's eyes sparkled teasingly.

"Honestly, I didn't want to lose it. I misplace things. And.. I was just 'practicing' for the wedding with friends." Abhay's expression turned sheepish.

Kavya raised an eyebrow, skepticism evident. Abhay's reaction didn't quite add up. Kavya wondered if there was more to the story.

"So Ravi saved the day, huh?" Kavya teased.

"Yup.. He did.. And boy, was he mad at me. He teased me, saying if it wasn't for him I'd be gone by now if you found out."

"I appreciate the honesty," Kavya chuckled. "This ring probably fell off someone's hand.."

Abhay nodded. "They might be searching for it. Maybe someone stopped by the stream for water and it slipped off."

He pocketed the ring, deciding it to turn it over to authorities once they returned to the city. As Abhay gazed the ring, memories flood back. "I was so nervous about our vows on the wedding day."

"Really? Buns, you seemed confident." Kavya said, surprised.

As they walked towards their car, Abhay reminisced about their wedding day. "We were worried it would rain, weren't we?" Abhay chuckled. "Luckily we had umbrellas and raincoats just in case."

"Oh yes! But the priest reassured us, saying rain on the wedding day brings blessings from above."

The golden rays were cast upon the picturesque venue, bathing the lush green gardens. Kavya's delicate footsteps echoed as she walked down the venue aisle, her family beside her. The soulful melody filled the air and Abhay's eyes locked onto Kavya's, his heart overflowing with emotions.

As they drove, Abhay and Kavya delved deeper into cherished memories. "Remember my uncle's dance moves, joined by your niece?" Abhay remembered.

As they exchanged vows, their vices trembled with sincerity. The ceremony concluded, sealing their union. At the reception, laughter and chatter filled the hall. The majestic wedding cake towered above the elegant centerpieces.

CHAPTER EIGHT

UNDERCURRENTS

The first dance brought gasps of admiration as Abhay and Kavya swayed to the romantic ballad. As the dance was coming to an end, Kavya's mind drifted back to the astrologer's words. "Be wary of water.. Its depths, superficial even.. Don't look at what's on the surface. Water has its undercurrents.. Be careful not to get stuck in one." She recalled Shreya's family astrologer, his piercing gaze and the unexpected warning. "You need to swim against the tides or else the undercurrents will pull you in." The memory sent shivers down her spine. Abhay noticed her discomfort and drew her closer.

"Hey, what's wrong?" He asked, whispering,

"Just feeling a little overwhelmed." Kavya said, unsure how to share the astrologer's ominous warning. She forced a smile.

"Daksh, is it?" Abhay's breath warm against her ear.

"Uhh.. Abhay, no? It has nothing to do with Daksh?" Her heart skipped a beat.

Abhay held her tight. "I know it's Daksh."

Kavya's eyes widened, panic rising. "Abhay, I don't know what to say to you--"

She had kept her secret meeting with Daksh hidden, along with her desire to uncover Abhay's past and the rumours surrounding him.

"Turn around," Abhay smiled mischievously.

Kavya obeyed and her eyes landed on Daksh, standing across the room, a warm smile on his face. Relief washed over her. Daksh had come to congratulate them.

"I thought so. He's hard to miss." Abhay chuckled.

Kavya's tension was replaced by gratitude for the misunderstanding.

Daksh approached, a warm smile on his face. "Congratulations, you two!"

Abhay thanked Daksh and gestured to the food counter, " Hey buddy, get something to eat and drink, catch up with others. We'll talk soon."

Daksh nodded and merged into the crowd, leaving Abhay and Kavya to their magical dance.

The night unfolded with merriment: the dances, the games, the speeches and delicious food. Kavya's thoughts lingered on Daksh's brief visit, wondering if Abhay suspected anything.

Shreya and Manish approached, beaming with congratulations. "I'm so happy for you both!" Shreya said, as she embraced them. "I'm so glad you had a karaoke night at your wedding." Shreya smiled warmly.

"Kavya's always been a karaoke enthusiast. She insisted on getting proposed to during a karaoke night." Abhay smiled mischievously.

"Wait, what? No, that's not true." Kavya's eyes widened.

"Oh come on, Kavya. Don't you remember? You said it had to be karaoke or nothing." Abhay chuckled.

"I didn't know you were planning a proposal, so I wouldn't know where you'd choose." Kavya said, as she shook her head.

Abhay winked and looked at Manish, "Had to oblige, do what the lady says."

Shreya's eyes narrowed slightly, sensing something off. "Didn't you guys get engaged at the bowling alley, where you first went on a date?"

"Actually, Kavya wanted to change venues. She was adamant about the bowling alley, said it held special memories." Abhay's expression turned innocent.

Kavya remembered suggesting the bowling alley, but Abhay had never mentioned a proposal.

Shreya looked at Abhay, relieved. "I remember how much Kavya hated karaoke. She would always end up singing the wrong lyrics and be embarrassed."

Abhay laughed. "Really? She's always had a secret love for karaoke."

Kavya's face hinted disagreement but Abhay continued.

"I had to convince her to keep it out of the main reception, but she finally agreed to a private session later."

Shreya's eyes sparkled with skepticism. "Really?"

Manish intervened, making the conversation lighter. "Anything you do for love, huh?"

Shreya smiled, playing along. "I suppose so. But some people take it too far."

"Guilty as charged." Abhay laughed.

Kavya's smile seemed strained, her eyes darting to Shreya. Shreya's gaze softened, her concern for Kavya evident. Abhay was busy with another guest.

"So, karaoke, huh?" Shreya probed.

"Don't, Shreya. I have no idea he'd say that." Kavya replied.

"Obviously, I know you," Shreya said. "Also, what's Daksh doing here? How's he mingling with Abhay and his friends?"

"Oh, Daksh is Abhay's schoolmate. They go way back," Kavya explained.

"The world's too small, isn't it?" Shreya observed.

"Yes, of course it is. Now don't look at him!" Kavya warned.

"Oopsie, he's coming here," Shreya whispered.

"Shreya, no!"

"Hey, Shreya Chandra? Is it?" Daksh asked, approaching.

"Yeah, hi Daksh. Long time no see," Shreya replied, with an awkward grin.

"Yeah, I know, right? Feels like a school and college reunion to me." Daksh said.

"Well, I was going to be here. Surprised you are here though. Didn't expect you to be here."

"Whoa, condescending as always, huh Shreya," Daksh remarked. "God, Kavya, why does she have a beef with me?"

"Shreya, cut it out, please,"; Kavya intervened. "And Daksh, do you have anything to say? I've been trying to reach you for a while. Did you find anything about Abhay's past?"

"Whoa, what's happening? Daksh is now Sherlock Holmes?" Shreya joked.

Kavya briefed Shreya about Abhay and she was now interested.

"Oh, sounds like blast from the past," Shreya said. "Why was I kept away from it, Kavya? We're close and you didn't tell me anything?" Shreya was mad.

"I'm sorry, Shreya. I didn't know what to make of it. The time wasn't right," Kavya apologized.

"It's alright, I understand.. How about we play a game of Truth and Dare?" Shreya suggested.

"Wow, Shreya, did you know, this is a wedding reception party and not your college annual event?" Daksh said sarcastically.

"Firstly, nobody's asking you to join," Shreya retorted. "Secondly, Kavya, this could be a great chance for us to get details from Abhay. We'll ask him questions about his past specifically. What do you say?"

"Yeah, and Abhay would spill it out in front of total strangers, things he's kept to himself for decades. Wow, Shreya, nice," Daksh said logically.

"And what suggestions do you have, Daksh? In fact, you were with Abhay when things happened, weren't you??"

"That was long time ago," Daksh replied. "I just happened to tell Kavya things while I was drunk."

"Typical Daksh. Typical."

"Enough, you guys," Kavya warned as she intervened. "Abhay's mom is approaching. Fight later, alright?"

"Ooh, she seems little tense," Shreya observed.

The group turned to see Abhay's mother approaching. "You're here! The bride is standing here without her husband?" Abhay's mother exclaimed. "You two are now married; you should be with each other. Now please come; I'll introduce you to Abhay's aunt, his favourite. She's been waiting to see you for a long time."

Kavya excused herself from the group and Abhay's mother escorted her towards his aunt. Kavya noticed the aunt, woman in her late 70s, struggling to stand straight, her once- perfect posture now compromised. Her grey hair was elegantly accessorized with pearl and gold clips.

As Kavya approached, the aunt waved, limping towards her while unclutching herself from her helper.

Abhay's mother introduced them.

"Hello, Nisha Aunty. It's lovely to finally meet you. Abhay told me all about you."

"Hello, Beta.. He really told you about me?"

"Yes, Auntie. How you helped him hide his report card in 6th grade, before his parents found out."

The aunt smiled, "Oh, yes. One little naughty boy he was.. or is, I'm not sure. I hardly get to see my people."

Kavya inquired about the aunt's health, noticing her smile gradually fading. The aunt's responses were cordial but curt, glancing at the family before speaking, as if coached.

"I don't know if I'll be around when you have kids," said Nisha aunty, pouting.

"Oh, no, Auntie. Why say that? Of course, you will be."

"You think so?" Nisha asked with a semi-smile.

"I know so," Kavya reassured.

Nisha thanked Kavya for her kind words and offered blessings. "It's a miracle I could attend Abhay's wedding."

As the helper prepared the ramp, Nisha gestured for Kavya to come closer for a hug. Whispering, she said, "Kavya, you're beautiful and intelligent. If only I were well.. I hope they allow you to live in peace. Things aren't as they appear. I hope Abhay.. Peace.. Find peace.."

The aunt gestured skyward and Abhay's family quickly escorted her back to the car. Her final words were muffled.

"I was fine before..Find peace..Things aren't what they look like, Beta."

Abhay's expression silenced Kavya's offer to help with the car door. They stood there, frozen in silence, until the car vanished into the distance. As they bid Nisha Auntie a poignant farewell, Kavya's mind lingered on the aunt's haunting words.

Abhay's eyes clouded, his gaze drifting away from Kavya's inquiring expression. "You know, my aunt's on medication," he said hastily, "and the care home wouldn't allow her at social events due to her condition."

"But what exactly happened to her?" Kavya's curiosity lingered.

Abhay's shoulder sagged, his voice barely above a whisper. "Schizophrenia and episodes of disruptive mood dysregulation disorder. After my uncle's passing, she became paranoid, quarreling with my family- especially my mom- for hours." He paused, collecting his thoughts.

"We tried to move her closer, but she refused. She's afraid we'll take away the farm, the only thing left of my uncle. It's understandable. My uncle and aunt raised my sister and me as their own."

Kavya's empathy deepened. "But why would she fear living next to you? Wouldn't it be comforting to have family nearby?"

Abhay's gaze fell. "The farm's all she had left of him. Our relationship's.. complicated." His voice cracked.

As they walked towards the kebab table, Abhay's expression shifted. "She was an athlete, strong and tall. She helped me through a tough time in school.." His voice trailed off.

"What happened back then?" Kavya's curiosity resurfaced.

"Just a wild fight. I wasn't always this calm."

Kavya sensed there was more, but Abhay's tone discouraged further inquiry. "Now isn't the time. He's already emotional." She thought.

"Now, let's grab those kebabs Ravi saved for us, before he gobbles them off!" Abhay said.

Kavya nodded, joining him at the table.

Ravi, Abhay's lifelong friend and neighbour, approached them with a platter of steaming kebabs. His messy black hair framed his lean, athletic face, and his bright eyes sparkled with mischief.

"Finally, the lovebirds!" Ravi exclaimed, distributing the kebabs unevenly, with a bigger share for Abhay. "I thought you two abandoned me for each other's company."

Abhay chuckled. "Ravi, you're ridiculous."

Ravi grinned, winking at Kavya. "Someone's got to keep things interesting. I saved the best kebabs for you both.. or should I say, for Abhay?"

Kavya laughed. "Ravi, you're so dramatic."

"Someone has to balance the seriousness around here. Besides, Abhay needs someone to keep him smiling." Ravi said.

Vikram, Ravi's and Abhay's friend, chimed in, "Ooooo... Roast!"

Abhay playfully rolled his eyes. "Ravi, stop."

"What? I'm just keeping things lively," Ravi's smile never wavered.

The group continued their lively banter, enjoying the kebabs and each other's company. As they enjoyed their kebabs, Priyanka approached, exchanging warm smiles with Kavya. "Hey, girl! Missed you."

"Priyanka! You're here!" Kavya hugged Priyanka. Vikram noticed Priyanka and his eyes lit up. "And who's this beautiful addition?"

Priyanka laughed, introducing herself. Vikram charmed Priyanka with his witty banter, and Ravi teased, "Vikram's got a new target!"

Vikram grinned. "Can't help it! Priyanka, join us. We're discussing life's essentials - kebabs and love."

"Sounds intriguing?" Priyanka smiled, taking a seat beside Kavya.

Vikram handed Priyanka a kebab. "Welcome to the chaos." Vikram introduced Priyanka to the rest of the group, his eyes sparkling with excitement.

"Vikram, would you like the next wedding to be yours, right here, right now, since the evening is young?" Kavya teased.

Vikram chuckled, gesturing to the flowers on the table, "Kavya, toss the bouquet. I'll catch it."

"It's the woman next in line who has to catch it, not the man." Kavya smiled and remarked. The group erupted into laughter.

Vikram turned to Priyanka. "Want to take a walk? We've had kebabs.. don't want any haddi, left to pick from our conversations."

"You're ridiculously smooth, Vikram," Priyanka said, smiling with amusement.

"Guilty as charged. But honestly, I'm just glad I can keep up with you." Vikram chuckled.

"I'm not sure I should be impressed or worried." Priyanka said, playfully.

"Definitely impressed. So, shall we?"

Priyanka nodded, smiling. As they stood up, the group cheered. "New couple alert!"

"Vikram's moving fast," Abhay chuckled.

"He's got game," Ravi said.

The group continued their lively chatter, speculating about Vikram and Priyanka's budding connection. Abhay excused himself as Ravi asked him to take a call. The network wasn't cooperating, so they stepped away to find a better signal. Meanwhile, Ankit and Asha, Ravi's girlfriend, engaged Kavya in conversation.

"Tell us about your family." Asha asked.

"There are three of us," Kavya replied. "Sometimes I imagine it could get overwhelming with siblings."

Asha nodded empathetically. "I'm an only child. I can imagine."

Ankit, listening in, chimed in, "I'm the middle child.. So a different perspective altogether."

Ankit turned to Kavya. "Have we met before?? You look familiar."

Kavya thought for a moment. "I don't recollect. This is our first time meeting."

The trio discussed movies, delved into their shared love for mainstream movies, discussing favourite actors.

"Ankit has a huge crush on Deepika Padukone. He met her once while he was vacationing in Mumbai, during the Bajirao Mastani promotions" Asha teased.

"That's amazing!" Kavya smiled.

"She's absolutely stunning. I was starstruck." Ankit's eyes sparkled.

"What was she like?"

Ankit's expression turned dreamy. "Elegant, intelligent, and beautiful - inside and out." Ankit grinned. "But I see a similar spark here.. a Bajirao Mastani like love story brewing."

Asha raised an eyebrow. "A love triangle, you mean?"

"Let's just say, the plot thickens. Soon, everyone will know who's who" Ankit whispered.

"What are you insinuating, Ankit?" Kavya asked. "Is this related to Vikram and Priyanka?"

Ankit's smile grew wider. "Maybe. Maybe not."

Asha leaned in. "Ankit, stop being mysterious."

Ankit's smile grew wider, leaving Kavya and Asha intrigued. They exchanged curious glances, mirroring each other's confusion. They wondered whether Ankit had lost his mind.

"Ankit's gone Bollywood." Asha rolled he eyes.

"Yeah. I think we should call him Bollywood Ankit." Kavya chuckled.

Abhay returned, ending the call. "All sorted," he said to Ravi.

"Who was it?" Kavya asked.

"My cousin, who wanted to congratulate me." Abhay replied.

Ankit slid into the conversation, grinning mischievously, "Ooo.. In time.."

"Shut up, Ankit." Asha said. "He's got Bollywood fever." She explained.

Ravi chuckled. "Ankit's plotting something?"

Asha waved her hand dismissively. "Ignore him. He thinks he's scripting our lives."

Abhay chuckled. "Ankit's lost it."

"Just enjoying the preview, my friends.." Ankit grinned.

Shreya, Manish and Daksh arrived at the table, preparing to leave.

Kavya asked, "Did you enjoy your meal and time?"

"We did, thanks." Shreya hugged Kavya.

Daksh exchanged a brief nod with Kavya. Ankit's gaze lingered on Daksh. "I've seen you somewhere recently..."

"Ankit asked me the same thing earlier," Kavya said.

"Maybe it's his icebreaker line." Abhay chuckled.

"Do you happen to own a Royal Enfield, Daksh?," quizzed Ankit.

"Yeah, I do.. Why? You wish to get one?"

"No reason, just curious. I've opened a restaurant near 5th lane, Solitaire Street. There's a tea stall next to it." Ankit said.

Kavya's eyes widened, her heart racing.

"The other day, a Royal Enfield was parked in front of my restaurant. There was a heated argument.. I remember now."

Daksh's expression turned cautious. "What argument?"

"Just a minor dispute concerning the parking. But I recall the rider's face... And the number plate." Ankit recalled.

"Ankit, drop it. Enough with your interrogation," said Ravi.

"No, I want to know. Was that you, Daksh?"

Abhay attempted to lighten the mood. "Even if it was him, what's the big deal? Many people park on the wrong side. Do you want compensation?"

Ankit clarified, "It's not about him and his bike; it's about the company he keeps while sipping tea."

"So what's wrong with the company I keep while sipping tea? Is it wrong to have tea now?" Daksh asked curiously.

"No, not at all." Ankit's gaze shifted to Kavya, intently, who stood anxiously nearby.

Shreya turned to Kavya, her voice sweet. "Kavya, could you help me find the restroom? I seem to have lost my way."

Kavya nodded, sensing a deeper reason behind Shreya's request. "Yes of course, let's go."

Shreya pulled Kavya into the restroom, her voice low. "Kavya,I don't like this. You're getting too close to Daksh."

"What's wrong with Daksh?"

"Remember the astrologer's warning? 'Beware of hidden truths?' I don't know why, I sensed something off."

"Shreya, you're being superstitious."

"Look, Abhay's past shrouded in mystery, now Daksh's involvement. Be cautious." Shreya said in a low whisper.

Meanwhile, outside, Ankit leaned in, his voice barely audible. "Abhay, I suspect Daksh meets Kavya near my restaurant."

"What are you insinuating, Ankit?" Abhay's expression turned stern.

"Just observing, Abhay. Kavya and Daksh seem evasive. I'm protecting my friends.." Ankit said.

Abhay's gaze turned serious. "Ankit, are you certain it was Kavya and Daksh?"

Ankit hesitated, his conviction wavering. "I.. I'm not entirely sure."

Abhay pressed on. "You're not sure? Then why suspect them?"

Ankit's voice dropped to a whisper. "Maybe I am mistaken. But the resemblance is uncanny."

Shreya and Kavya stepped out of the restroom, rejoining the group.

Shreya glanced at Daksh. "We should head out."

Daksh nodded in agreement. "Yes, it's getting late."

Shreya turned to her husband. "Manish, are you ready?"

Manish, engrossed in his phone, looked up. "Yeah, let's go."

They exchanged pleasantries, Shreya locked eyes with Kavya, her eyes conveying a silent message of protection and warning. Daksh, too, glanced at Kavya, his expression unreadable. Ankit's eyes darted between them, his mind still racing to place the familiar scene.

Abhay, oblivious, smiled warmly. Let's grab dessert."

As they walked to the dessert section, Kavya's phone buzzed in her purse. She excused herself to check. Daksh's message flashed on the screen:

Daksh: "Kavya, we shouldn't meet anymore. Too risky. I'll contact you only when I have something concrete"

Kavya felt a mix of relief and anxiety. She deleted the message, ensuring no digital trail. Returning to Abhay and the group, she wore a mask of calmness. She would wait for Daksh's message, no matter how long.

CHAPTER NINE

LAKESIDE VIEW

Kavya's eyes narrowed at the GPS screen, her brow furrowed in confusion. "This can't be right," she muttered, glancing at Abhay, who was navigating the winding road with ease.

"Maybe it's just a glitch," Abhay replied, his sight flicking between the road and the screen. "Let's see where it takes us."

As they rounded a bend, a narrow path materialized before them. Towering trees lined the route, the gravelly surface seemed to beckon them, and Abhay turned the wheel, steering the car onto the mysterious trail. The crunch of gravel beneath their tyres filled the air as they ventured deeper into the woods.

"Where do you think this leads?" Kavya asked curiously.

"Only one way to find out." Abhay's eyes sparkled with adventure.

The path twisted and turned, the trees growing denser, filtering the sunlight. Suddenly, the woods parted, revealing a breathtaking vista. A serene lake stretched before them, its glassy surface mirroring the vibrant hues of the surrounding foliage.

Kavya gasped, her hand flying to her mouth. Abhay slammed on the brakes and they sat in silence, taking in the unexpected beauty. As they stepped out of the car, the only sounds were the gentle lapping of the water against the shore and the chirping of the birds. They wandered towards the lake's edge, their eyes locked on the perfect reflection of the trees. Abhay, his arms brushing against hers. "I guess the GPS had a surprise in store for us," he said, his voice filled with wonder.

Kavya turned to him, "And what other secrets do you think are hiding beyond the mirage?"

Abhay's eyes already scanning the surrounding woods, eager to uncover the next mystery. Together, they stood there, the tranquility of the lake enveloping them, as they contemplated the adventures that lay ahead.

Kavya's eyes scanned the familiar lakeside setting, unease creeping over her. Eight months ago, Abhay had brought her to a similar spot, and the memories still sent shivers down her spine.

"Isn't it breathtaking?" Abhay asked. His voice low and hypnotic.

Kavya's heart quickened as she took in the eerie similarities to their past date: the picturesque restaurant, the similar lake pier, and the same isolation. The sun was setting, casting an orange glow across the lake's surface.

"Let's take a walk," Abhay suggested, his eyes never leaving the water.

Kavya hesitated, her fear of water resurfacing. "I'd rather stay here," she replied, trying to sound casual.

"Come on, it'll be an adventure," Abhay turned to her, his smile knowing.

"What kind of adventure?" She asked.

"You'll see," Abhay chuckled. He offered his hand.

Kavya's instincts screamed at her to refuse but she took his hand, her palm sweating. As they walked towards the pier, the silence between them grew thicker. Kavya's senses heightened, her eyes scanning the surrounding area.

The familiar words echoed in her mind: "I like the calmness of the water.. Lakes are better. Their waves don't make a sound. On the surface its quiet, but there's currents brewing underneath."

Eight months ago, he had spoken these same words, lost in thought, forgetting she stood beside him. "Nobody around, in solitude.. It's like the quiet before the storm." Kavya then quickly snapped him out of his reverie, citing her parents' worry as she was getting late.

Now, as they stood at a similar spot, Kavya's unease deepened. Why had he brought her here? Was it intentional, knowing she couldn't swim? Abhay's enchantment with the lake unsettled her.

As he removed his shirt, revealing the "RH" tattoo on his arm. 'Riya Hari', his ex-girlfriend, flashed into Kavya's mind. Dark- haired, lean and melodious - voiced, Riya had captivated everyone, especially Abhay's mother.

"Abhay, why are you evasive about moving out?" Kavya asked, her voice firm. "Why do you want to stay back here?"

Abhay was guarded. "Paperwork, documentation.. It takes time. Give me some time. We'll move when things are ready."

CHAPTER TEN

RUMOUR HAS IT...

Kavya remembered groggily opening her eyes, greeted by a severe headache. The murmur of voices from the living room pierced through her pain. Women were chatting in hushed, excited tones, their giggles carrying across the hall. She tossed the blanket and swung her legs over the side of the bed, wincing as her head throbbed. Desperate for relief, she shuffled to the kitchen to warm up some milk. The conversation could be heard in hushed tones.

"Where is she now?" One woman asked.

"Sleeping, I presume," another replied, directing the question to Abhay's mother.

"Yes, she doesn't know you'll are here. Must be sleeping," Abhay's mother confirmed.

An older woman, possibly in her late 70s, spoke up, "Does she do the chores?"

"Well, she's a bit slothful. You know how these young women are nowadays.." Abhay's mother replied.

The older lady chimed in, her tone patronizing, "Wouldn't it be great if Abhay had married Riya instead?"

"I do wonder that myself," Abhay's mother sighed wistfully.

Another woman added, "Heard she's back from Canada and wishes to reside here again. Such a lovely soul. She would keep in touch while she was in Canada and even offered me to visit her there. If only my knees could cope with the weather there...'

Abhay's mother nodded enthusiastically. "Yes, Riya always had a way of connecting with people."

"I wonder what made her move to Canada suddenly? And even Abhay stayed back when everything was finalized."

Abhay's mother leaned in, her curiosity evident. "Riya never really wanted to move there, but she agreed because of Abhay. And look now, she's thriving there."

"Maybe it was because of the break up?" On of the women pondered.

"Still, it's strange.. Abhay seemed so committed to her. But they said it was mutual, no hard feelings."

The older woman's voice tinged with nostalgia repeated, "They were perfect together."

Kavya, still listening from the kitchen, felt a pang of unease. Abhay's feelings for Riya felt complex. Her mind reeled as she processed the conversation. Riya's return and potential reunion with Abhay unsettled her.

Now, as she was standing near the lake beside Abhay, her mind racing with connections, she turned to face him. "Abhay, is your reluctance to move out because Riya is back in town?"

"What makes you think that?" He asked, his tone curious.

"The 'RH' tattoo and your mother's conversation.. It's all connected, isn't it?"

Abhay's silence spoke volumes.

"Abhay, answer me," Kavya pressed, her voice unwavering.

"Kavya, it's complicated," he began, his voice low.

"Then make me understand!" Kavya urged, frustration etching her face."Is Riya the reason behind your school fight?"

"Why do you always bring up that fight?" His expression darkened.

"Because you've been evasive, Abhay," Kavya said, her voice trembling. "You keep secrets from me. I want to know the truth."

Abhay's face twisted in rage, his eyes blazing. "Oh, I'm the one keeping secrets? You're the one meeting Daksh in secret, talking to him behind my back."

Kavya's eyes widened as Abhay's grip on her arm tightened, his fingers digging into her skin.

"How did you...?" She stammered.

"My mother told me," Abhay growled, his voice menacing.

Suddenly, memories flooded Kavya's mind. That fateful day, after Abhay's mother and friends left, Kavya was alone in the house. She brewed a cup of tea in the kitchen, thinking Abhay's mother was outside. As she turned on the music, her phone pinged. A voice note from Daksh.

"Hey Kavya, I'm sorry I'm out for work in Delhi. Will be in town soon. Heard Abhay's not in town. I really want to talk to you.. Let me know once you're free. I---"

Kavya frozen. Abhay's mother stood before her, disappointment etched on her face.

Kavya tried to shake off his grip, but Abhay held firm, his anger radiating like a palpable force.

"You don't trust me, do you?? Always assuming things, asking others about me instead of talking to me directly."

Abhay's face was inches from hers.

Kavya's fear spiked as Abhay's hot breath danced across her skin. She felt trapped, unsure if he'd harm her.

"Abhay, please..." She whispered, trying to reason with him.

CHAPTER ELEVEN

THE SOUND OF TROUBLE

Kavya looked into Abhay's eyes, red-rimmed and desperate but also seemed vulnerable. Kavya sensed a depth of turmoil on his face. Just as he was about to release her, their car's horn blared, shattering the tense silence.

The sudden sound made them both jump. Kavya noticed as Abhay's arm instinctively dropped from her arm. "Who...?" Kavya's gaze darting towards the car.

Abhay's face twisted in confusion. "Impossible. The car's locked."

The horn continued, piercing the stillness. Blonk. Blonk. Blonk.

Kavya took a step back, her eyes fixed on the car. ""This can't be happening."

"Someone's playing a sick joke," Abhay muttered.

But as they scanned their surroundings, they realized:

They were alone. No figures in the shadows. No movement stirred the trees. The horn's incessant blaring seemed to take on an eerie quality. Kavya's skin crawled. "I want to get out of here."

Abhay's eyes were fixed on the car, his jaw clenched. Suddenly, the horn fell silent. The stillness that followed was oppressive. Abhay strode towards the car, his eyes scanning the surroundings.

"I'll check the tyres." He said.

Kavya followed him, "What's going on?"

Abhay knelt beside the front tyre, his expression tightening. "This can't be."

"What's it?" Kavya peered over his shoulder.

"The tyre's punctured," Abhay said, incredulity etched on his face.

"But it was fine earlier."

Abhay's eyes swept the area, his eyes narrowing. 'Nobody's around. No sign of pranksters."

An unsettling silence fell between them. Was Abhay orchestrating this? Was Kavya behind this? Their eyes met, suspicion lingering between them.

"Looks like someone's playing games with us." Abhay said, his tone neutral.

"But who?" Kavya asked.

"Maybe we should ask ourselves." Abhay said, seemingly suspecting Kavya.

"We should check inside the car, see if anything's stolen," Kavya suggested, scanning the car on the inside.

Abhay nodded, already opening the door. "Nothing's stolen, I checked. There's no reason for the horn to blare. It's all so weird."

"Maybe someone messed with the wiring?"

Abhay shook his head. "No signs of tampering. It's as if.. something just triggered the horn."

The interior of the car seemed undisturbed, yet a haunting feeling remained.

"Do you think someone's watching us?"

"I don't know, but I don't like it."

As they stood beside he car, Post Malone's 'Circles‘ suddenly filled the air.

Maybe you don't understand what I'm going through
It's only me
What you got to lose?
Make up your mind, tell me
What are you gonna do?

"How's the stereo working, Abhay?"

Abhay's expression remained impassive, but his eyes flickered with unease.

It's only me
Let it go

The lyrics hung in the air, echoing their tense standoff.

"This is surreal," Kavya whispered.

"Just a weird coincidence," Abhay thought.

Make up your mind, tell me
What are you gonna do?

They searched each other's eyes. The music continued, weaving an unsettling atmosphere. Suddenly, Kavya reached into the car and pulled the AUX cord out of the stereo. The music stopped abruptly.

As they walked, Google Maps guiding them to a garage 2 km away, their minds wandered. Kavya revisited what just happened some time ago. The astrologer's warning: "Beware of the depths of water."

Abhay's thoughts drifted to Ankit's caution: "Kavya has been secretly meeting Daksh." Doubts resurfaced. Kavya's flashback intensified:

Abhay's piercing words: "My mom overheard you talking to Daksh." The suspicion in his eyes. The confusion: 'Stay away from Daksh, yet invite him to the wedding.'

CHAPTER TWELVE

DIGGING THE GRAVE

Kavya remembered how she gathered her thoughts, ready to talk to Abhay. "Abhay, I need to ask you something."

"Of course, what's it?" Abhay replied.

"Look, I'm confused about----" Just as Kavya began, Abhay's phone buzzed. Ravi's text, followed by a call.

"Sorry, I need to take this," Abhay said, his expression shifting.

Abhay's voice dropped to a whisper. He listened intently, his face falling.

"What happened?" Kavya asked.

"I need to take this call in private," Abhay said, stepping into another room. Minutes passed. Abhay returned, packing his bag with urgency.

"What's wrong?" Kavya asked, concerned.

"My colleague.. died of cardiac arrest. Ravi called me to attend the funeral." Abhay was shocked. "Mid- 30s, wife, young child.. It's devastating," Abhay continued.

Kavya's concern shifted from Daksh to Abhay's distress. She reached out, touching his arm. "I'm so sorry, Abhay."

"Thanks, Kavya. I...need to go." Abhay said, his eyes still clouded.

Kavya nodded. Their conversation about Daksh was forgotten. Kavya noticed Abhay's wallet, she picked it up, possibly forgotten in haste. She dialled his number, but it went straight to voicemail.

"Abhay, you left your wallet. Call me back."

No response. Her concern grew. She scrolled through Abhay's contacts, searching for an alternative. Varun, Abhay's colleague was listed. She called Varun.

"Hey, Kavya. What's up?" Varun answered.

"Hi Varun. Sorry to bother you. Abhay received a call from Ravi about a colleague's funeral and rushed out. He forgot his wallet. Could you please---"

"Funeral? What colleague?" Varun's tone shifted from casual to confused.

"Abhay said Ravi called him about a colleague's cardiac arrest.. He was quite young, in his mid-30s.. has a young child.."

Varun's silence was telling. "I don't know anything about a funeral, Kavya and I'm definitely not attending one."

Kavya's doubt escalated.

"Maybe there's someone from another team who's passed away and I'm not aware... Abhay is friends with people from other departments too. Please don't worry, I'll ask someone to call Abhay. Do you want me to come and pick the wallet, Kavya?"

"Thank you, Varun, but I guess I'll wait for a few minutes, maybe Abhay will return, noticing his missing wallet."

"Alright, Kavya. I'm sorry I couldn't be of much help... I'll also ask someone to call Ravi, since he could be with Abhay." Varun's empathy was palpable.

"I've been trying Ravi too, but his number is busy."

"Try calling Abhay's office landline. Maybe someone there knows something," Varun suggested.

"Thanks Varun, I'll try calling there."

As they hung up, Kavya's discomfort grew. Where was Abhay really?

CHAPTER THIRTEEN

LOST AND FOUND?

Kavya glanced at Google Maps. "200 meters to the garage," she said.

Abhay squinted at the screen. "But look, it says there's a Dhaba nearby." He scanned the surroundings. "I don't see any Dhaba."

A fruit vendor nearby arranged his wares. Noticing their confusion, he approached.

"Let's ask him," Abhay suggested.

"Need directions?" Asked the fruit vendor, smiling.

"Is there a garage nearby?" Abhay asked.

"Yes, you see that street there? Take a left, you'll meet a crossroad. Keep taking left until the end of the street." The vendor pointed, gesturing down the street.

Kavya pulled out her phone, rechecking Google Maps. "This doesn't match," she said, raising her eyebrow.

"Maps can't replace local knowledge, Tai." The vendor said with a smile.

"Got it, thanks" Abhay said nodding, memorizing the road.

The vendor, noticing their fatigue, offered them fruits. "Take some fruits for the road. You must be hungry." He handed them a few apples, bananas and grapes. "Refresh yourselves."

Abhay pulled out his wallet. "I'll pay for the fruits," he said, handing them to Kavya.

The vendor's hands waved dismissively. "No, no, take them as a gift."

Kavya and Abhay exchanged awkward glances. "But Kaka, it's too kind of you---," Kavya protested.

"Next time you're around, come visit. Then I'll take money from you." The vendor smiled warmly.

Abhay and Kavya nodded. "Thank you, we will," they replied.

As they walked, Kavya glanced back, the fruit vendor still looking at them. "That was strange, no?"

'Yeah, but it was kind of him," Abhay said.

Their walks continued, the fruits' sweetness lingering. The streets seemed increasingly deserted. The buildings grew older, worn. Abhay scratched his head. "Keep left until the end of the street.." he repeated.

Kavya shielded her eyes from the scorching sun. "How long are we supposed to walk?"

"Google Maps deceived us yet again. Thought it'll be 200 meters only." She said in frustration.

"Maybe we missed a turn," Abhay consulted the vendor's directions.

The endless stretch of deserted street loomed before them. No signs of life, no sounds of civilization. Just the blistering sun and their weary footsteps.

"What kind of a place is this?"

"I don't know, but let's keep moving."

The stench of decay intensified as they navigated the potholed road.

"Is that a sewage drain nearby?" Kavya covered her nose.

A dilapidated hut loomed before them, a testament to neglect. Ripped sofa cushions littered the ground, rat gnaw-marks visible. Windows, partially closed, wore thick webs like icy veils. The roof sagged, as if weighed down by years of abandonment. A faint scent of paan and stale air clung to the structure.

"Oh, no! Look! We're back at the same spot." Kavya said, in an alarming tone.

"We've come a full circle.." Abhay muttered.

"The diversion! The police asked us to take this route because of construction work in progress." Kavya's frustration boiled over.

"I know these roads like the back of my hand.. but this diversion.. I don't understand." Abhay's brow furrowed.

"Why can't we find the garage?" Kavya's voice trembled.

"We need to keep moving. We can't give up." Abhay's eyes scanned the horizon. Was it bad luck or something sinister? As they stood at the crossroads, the forest loomed behind them. The highway beckoned, a promise of civilization. But was it the path that will lead them to safety?

As they walked towards the highway, Abhay's voice filled with emotion. "I want to stay in the city, Kavya.. My heart belongs here."

"Because Riya Hari's back, isn't she?" Kavya asked.

Abhay's expression faltered. "What makes you think.. I just found out from you that she's moved back. It has nothing to do with Riya.."

"And the 'sudden death' of your colleague? I know about your colleague and the 'funeral'.." Kavya said in a cryptic tone.

"You think I lied about the funeral?? I was there, Kavya, I paid my respects." Abhay was anguished. Tears ran down Abhay's face. "You're being insensitive..."

Had Kavya misjudged Abhay? But Varun's words echoed in her mind. "Varun didn't know about the colleague's death," Kavya countered.

Abhay stepped closer, his eyes locked with Kavya's. "Where are you heading with these accusations, Kavya?" He asked intensely.

"Anyway, let me explain.." Abhay's voice dropped to a whisper.

CHAPTER FOURTEEN

THREADS THAT BIND

Abhay's narrative unfolded. "Riya Hari, my childhood sweetheart.. she's ambitious. She wanted to move to Canada, but it put a financial burden on me. I had to take two jobs.. it was unsustainable."

"We broke up, mutually. Financial reasons. My aunt needed me here.." Abhay's sincerity seemed genuine. "Let's focus on getting out of here." Abhay pleaded.

Kavya nodded, her resolve renewed. Together, they walked towards the highway. Abhay's secrets, it seemed, were slowly unraveling. Kavya recalled her encounter at the supermarket. Rattling carts and baskets filled the air.

"Why don't they restock these shelves?" Kavya muttered.

She navigated the the narrow aisle, dodging shoppers. Her cart tangled with a woman's, who apologized. "I'm so sorry, I didn't realize."

"It's alright. The aisles are quite narrow." Kavya smiled warmly.

As Kavya left for checkout, the woman asked :

"Hey, are you Kavya Apte? Abhay's wife?"

"Yes, I am. Sorry, I didn't recognise you." Kavya tried to recollect.

"I should've introduced myself earlier." Congratulatory words flowed. "I'm Riya Hari."

"I saw your photos on the social media. Abhay's lucky." Riya cooed.

Kavya's politeness hid her unease.

"Oh no, I forgot the dark Toblerone bar.. I better rush to grab it before the checkout line gets longer."

Riya's eyes sparkled with amusement. "Abhay's favourite. Toblerone bar. I can now see why he loves you."

Their shared laughter was awkward. Riya continued, "I hope Abhay eats the chocolate.. instead of sharing it with someone else.."

"What do you mean? Sharing it with someone else?" Kavya asked, confused.

"You know Abhay. He has this weird habit of giving away the gifts he receives. I never understood. When we were together, I'd gift him things, but they'd vanish."

The fluorescent lights pulsed above, casting an eerie glow. Kavya pressed Riya for more information.

"I've always wondered," Riya said, her voice mixed with skepticism, "why someone wouldn't keep gifts they liked. Did Abhay truly appreciate them, or was it just a facade?"

Kavya's mind flashed back to their wedding day. Abhay had opened gifts in her absence, dismissively calling it "cleaning the clutter." A memory resurfaced- Abhay giving away the beautiful moon lamp gifted to them, claiming they wouldn't need it.

"How are you doing, Riya?"

"I'm doing well in Quebec. Starting my new business was challenging. Honestly, I never thought I'd adjust to life away from India, but I've managed."

"Why did you hesitate to move?"

"I never wanted to leave India, but Abhay insisted on moving to Canada. Thankfully, his uncle helped us with the paperwork, and we owe him a lot." Riya turned nostalgic.

"His uncle? Was he around that time?"

Riya nodded. "Yes, of course! His aunt would often accompany us. I'm sorry to hear about his uncle's passing. How's his aunt doing now? I should have reached out after his uncle passed.. Life got busy."

"She's receiving treatment now. Thanks for asking." Kavya, wanting to leave but was in a dilemma, stopped and continued, "Riya, can I ask you something?"

Riya nodded, her expression guarded.

"Why did you really break up with Abhay?" Kavya asked bluntly.

"We wanted different things.. Abhay's priorities changed. Abhay's focus changed from us to.. other things." Riya said with a tinge of sadness. "Did something happen, Kavya? You're asking me about us.."

"No, nothing happened, Riya. I just wanted to know about it.. I'm sorry if it came out this way..."

"I never really understood Abhay," Riya was being contemplative. "He could be loving one moment and cold the next. Nobody really knows what went on his mind. Now that you're his wife, I'm sure he's past those things. He's a good guy, Kavya."

"Riya, can I ask you something else?"

"Of course."

"What happened at school? Specifically, the fight against the boys from other school that landed him in rehab?"

"To be honest, I don't recall the details. Abhay mentioned it was something 'between the boys'. Ravi said it might have been over a love interest that escalated into something else."

"Alright, thanks.."

"Abhay's behaviour changed after that incident. He became.. guarded. Like he was---"

"Hiding something?" Kavya finished Riya's sentence.

Riya nodded. "But why bring it up now, Kavya?"

"No, I just always wondered if you were involved in the fight somehow, was it about you.."

"No, not at all. I too, searched for answers back then, but we've grown up, and I never thought about it again." Riya shrugged, with a mix of curiosity and concern in her eyes.

CHAPTER FIFTEEN

THE LEGEND OF CHAKWA

Kavya walked alongside Abhay towards the highway. His words contradicted Riya's narrative, fueling her doubts. Abhay confidently navigated the roads, refusing to ask police personnel for directions. As they walked, hunger and exhaustion set in. They stopped at a deserted tin- covered kiosk, surrounded by dated newspapers. A rugged young man approached, dusty trousers and mud- stained T- shirt clinging to his frame. His curious and perturbed expression made them uneasy.

"Oye! Oye!" He yelled from a distance.

Kavya and Abhay hastily packed their belongings, thinking he mistook them for trespassers.

"Wait! Don't leave.." He painted, wiping sweat fom his face.

The man pointed to the kiosk's signboard: 'Gurunath Garage's

"What brings you here?" Guru asked.

"Our car's tyre punctured," Abhay explained.

"Where's your car?" Guru's eyes narrowed.

"Near the lake.. inside the forest," Kavya replied.

Guru turned serious. "Inside the forest? Alright, hop on, we'll go in my pickup truck."

Kavya and Abhay shared uncertain glances.

"Sir Ji, I'm the only mechanic here. This is my garage, running for decades.. Trust me, look," Guru reassured, showing his identity card.

"Can we trust him?" Kavya whispered to Abhay.

"We have no choice," Abhay nodded.

As they hesitated, Guru turned to them, encouraging,"Come, Tai, I'll fix your car. You won't find anyone else around here."

They hopped into his rusty pickup truck, the worn seats cracking beneath them. "Hold on tight, Dada. The forest roads can get rough." Guru warned.

Abhay nodded. As the truck navigated the winding roads, Guru asked, "So, what brings you folks to these parts?"

"Just a gateway. We wanted some peace, away from the city." Abhay replied.

"And you're newly married, I assume?" Guru asked, eyes sparkling with curiosity. Kavya felt a twinge of discomfort at the intrusive question.

"Don't get me wrong, Tai, it's just that many newly married couples do 'lose their way' in the forest." Guru said with a smirk.

"We have truly lost our way. We thought we found the road, but lost it again. We were near a well and followed the path near he lakeside. Then, someone played a prank on us, our wires got messed up and the tyre got punctured." Abhay narrated.

"Wait, what well are you talking about?"

"The covered well," Kavya explained. "It was dry, but surprisingly had fresh water flowing next to it."

'It was an old one, covered with foliage, with a wooden lid. Thankfully, we didn't fall into it." Abhay said, with a sigh of relief. Kavya, too, nodded.

"Dada, are you sure it was a well?" Guru asked with confusion.

"Yes," Abhay and Kavya replied in unison.

Guru's eyes widened. "I've been here since long, and I've never encountered a well or heard anyone mention one."

Abhay and Kavya gasped in unison. Abhay dismissed Guru's claims with a chuckle. "The next thing you'll say is that the forest doesn't exist."

"No, Dada. I swear to God, this forest and Holabhadrasht Nagar have their secrets."

"What secrets?" Kavya inquired.

Guru's eyes seemed to cloud over. "This village has always been hub for mysterious events. I remember when I was new here, a group of researchers arrived to study the rare Karvi shrubs. They stumbled upon a group of hares and peacocks, which was unusual, given the presence of predators like leopards in the area."

"What happened next?" Kavya said, leaning in, intrigued.

"They captured the animals on camera for a documentary, but when they reviewed the footage, the images and videos were blank. Nothing was visible on the cameras."

"That's exactly what happened to me! I took pictures, but they didn't show up on my phone." Kavya's eyes widened, as she looked at Abhay.

Abhay cut in, his tone skeptical. "Villages are often filled with legends and myths. We should be cautious of exaggeration."

"Dada, I don't claim to have experienced anything paranormal myself. However, after that incident, many villagers stopped tourists from visiting the forest. In fact, many villagers were against the researchers entering the forest. They ignored the cautions and had to bear the consequences..."

"What consequences?" Abhay asked, wanting to know more.

"They were never seen again. Their equipment, their cameras, everything was found later, but they vanished into thin air."

Abhay and Kavya were stupefied. "That's ridiculous. There must be a logical explanation." Abhay's skepticism returned.

"I'm just telling you'll what happened.. Some say that time works differently here. The forest plays tricks on people's minds.." Guru's body language was sombre. "You'll are city folks, Dada and Tai, you'll never believe us. But there are certain things beyond our imagination. Do you'll know, there's Chakwa that works here."

"Chakwa? What's that?" Kavya asked.

"Chakwa is a phenomenon where time becomes.. fluid. It's as if the path has a mind of its own, and it can manipulate time to repeat itself."

"Impossible. Time is a linear concept." Kavya said, unable to grasp.

"Not in this forest. Here, time is a cycle. And once you're trapped in the Chakwa, you'll relive the same moments over and over."

"Relive the same moments? What do you mean?" Abhay's interest piqued.

Guru's voice was now a whisper. "I mean that you'll experience the same events, the same conversations, the same everything. But each time, it'll be a slightly different. And you'll never be able to escape the cycle. It's an ancient thing, been happening in these woods for centuries."

"It's just a myth.." Abhay was firm, his arms crossed over his chest. "If that's the case, how did Kavya and I manage to come out of the forest and find your garage? And also, nothing has repeated with us."

"One shouldn't dismiss the old ways, Dada. This forest has a power you can't understand." Guru's hand remained on the steering wheel, his face still turned back towards Abhay and Kavya. The silence was oppressive, weighing heavily on Abhay's and Kavya's minds. Guru's gesture, inscrutable, his eyes fixed on the road ahead. The only sounds was the creaking of the truck's old wooden frame, the snapping of the twigs and branches and a distant call of a bird.

Suddenly, Guru's voice broke the silence. "We're here," he said, his voice low and gravelly. As the truck came to a stop, Abhay and Kavya looked at each other, their hearts racing with anticipation. What lay ahead for them in this strange and foreboding forest?

"Is this your car?" Guru asked.

"Yes, it is," Abhay replied.

Guru nodded. "Okay, I'll go check the tyres and see what other repairs need to be done." He grabbed his toolbox from the truck's seat compartment.

"I'll come along," Abhay said, turning to Kavya. "You wait here, okay?"

Kavya nodded, watching as Abhay and Guru walked towards their car. They seemed to be engrossed in conversation, their voices carrying on the wind. As they approached the car, Abhay asked Guru, "What tool you're carrying?"

Guru held up a wrench. "This is a tyre iron. It's used to loosen the lug nuts on the wheel."

"I've never seen one like that before. How does it work?"

Guru smiled, happy to explain. "It's simple, really. You just place the iron on the lug nuts and turn it counterclockwise..."

As Guru inspected the car, Abhay leaned in, their conversation hushed and indistinct. Kavya watched them for a moment, her eyes squinting slightly in the fading light. Just then, a cool breeze rustled the leaves behind her, carrying a faint whisper. Kavya turned to face the wind, but there was nothing to see. Her phone vibrated in her hand, breaking the spell. Kavya was surprised as she stared the screen. 17 missed calls and 8 messages from Daksh? And a couple of them from an unknown number? Her mind racing, she wondered what could be so urgent. Daksh never called her this many times unless it was an emergency. And who could be calling her from an unknown number? Kavya's thumb hovered over the screen, hesitating.

Kavya stood there, contemplating whether to answer the call or messages. She glanced over at Abhay and Guru, who seemed engrossed in something related to the car. Her eyes then returned to her phone, where she saw a string of messages from Daksh.

CHAPTER SIXTEEN

MAYDAY MAYDAY

The messages read:

11:27: Hey

12:02: Hey, I wanted to talk to you. Let me know when you're free.

13:47: It's kinda urgent..

13:56: Kavya??

14:50: WHERE ARE YOU? ARE YOU ALRIGHT?

15:21: I'm leaving...

15:27: Nobody at home? Your phone is switched off? Kavya?

16:24: I'm unable to reach Abhay too.. I'm worried. WHAT HAPPENED?

As Kavya finished reading the messages, she wanted to check the unknown caller. But before she could, her phone rang again, the vibration loud and insistent. Kavya quickly tried to hush the phone by covering it with her hand. She walked a short distance away, far enough to keep an eye on Abhay and Guru in case they approached. She stared at the unknown number on the screen.

"Hello?" Kavya whispered.

There was a pause on the other end of the line, and for a moment, Kavya wondered if the call had dropped.

"Finally, Kavya, where are you?" Daksh said, his voice a mix of worry and relief.

"Hi, Daksh.. I just read your messages," Kavya replied, trying to process the flurry of emotions.

"Alright, read them later. Listen to me, Kavya. Is Abhay nearby?" Daksh asked, his tone urgent.

Kavya glanced around, ensuring Abhay was still out of earshot. "Umm.. Not at the moment, actually. Why? You wish to speak to him?"

"No, Kavya. I thought something terrible happened to you..given Abhay's anger," Daksh explained, with concern in his voice. "Anyway, I also tried getting my cousin, who's a Public Safety Officer. This is her number. Save it."

Kavya heard the Officer's voice in the background, asking Daksh to ask Kavya her location. "Daksh, I have no idea where I am.. That's the thing, I think we've lost our way. There's a lake... Umm.. Yeah! Somewhere around Holabhadrasht Nagar," Kavya replied, trying to recall any distinctive landmarks. She heard Daksh repeating the location to the Officer.

"Kavya, we can talk later, but my cousin wishes to speak to you. Don't hang up!" Daksh warned, with a firm voice.

"Daksh, that's not necessary---" Kavya protested.

"Hi, Kavya. I'm Officer Divya Gupta. Please tell me what can you see around you?", a firm authoritative voice interrupted.

Kavya took a deep breath, trying to process the sudden change in the conversation. "Umm.. Officer, I can see a lot of trees, to be honest. The maps are deceiving.. and we had our tyre punctured, so we got a mechanic who's repairing our car right now."

"Does the mechanic seem suspicious?" Officer Gupta asked.

"No, ma'am. We saw his identity card," Kavya reassured the Officer.

"Alright, anything else you can share?" Officer Gupta pressed on.

"Gurunath Garage seems miles away from where we are.. possibly a 35/40 minute dive?" Kavya offered relevant details.

"Okay.. my team will get there soon. Please stay safe, and avoid any confrontation that could land you in trouble. We will handle it once we get there. Do you have any spray or equipment for safety?" Officer Gupta instructed.

"Yes, Officer, I do," Kavya said, feeling a sense of relief wash over her.

"Alright, good. I've noted down your coordinates. Stay on the line, and we'll keep you updated on our ETA," Officer Gupta said, her voice firm and reassuring.

"Thank you, Officer." Kavya felt a sense of gratitude towards Officer Gupta.

"Kavya, I need to talk to you" Daksh urged. "Please listen to me."

"I'm listening, Daksh. What's it?"

Daksh's voice was a mx of emotions- concern, relief and a hint of curiosity. "Kavya, I finally have answers about Abhay's past, about the school fight. You won't believe what I found out."

"Really, finally!" Kavya exclaimed, trying to keep her voice down.

For almost five minutes, Kavya listened intently to Daksh's words, her phone pressed tightly against her ear. Her expression reflected denial and shock. "That's unbelievable. You're not serious, are you?"

But Daksh was dead serious. "Kavya, I'm telling you, this is what Riya told me. And it all makes sense, if you think about it. Abhay's behaviour, his mood swings... It all adds up."

As Daksh continued, Kavya's mind was racing, she connected the dots. Ravi asking for immigration help, Abhay's sudden change of heart about moving, the moon lamp, the custom- made cufflinks.. it all made sense now."

"Enough, I've heard it all," Kavya said, trying to process everything. "You better be sure of all this, alright?" Just then, she sensed a warm breath behind her. A shadow loomed, cast by the almost-dusk sun, still and unmoving. Kavya knew the truth; she had finally connected the dots.

Sensing no reply no reply from Kavya, Daksh said, "Kavya, don't hang up! I'm recording this call!"

Kavya turned around, her phone still in hand, her expression stumped. Abhay stood before her, a pliers wrench in his hand, his eyes boring her soul. There was silence as Abhay stared at Kavya. This time, Kavya knew the answers; this time, she know what Abhay would say. This time, she couldn't be fooled.

"Be sure of what, Kavya?" Abhay asked.

"Sorry?" Kavya replied, unsure.

"You're on call with someone? You said they better be sure of something... Be sure of what? Who's it?" Abhay pressed. He held the pliers, rubbing the dirt off them.

Kavya hesitated before responding. "The... I dialled an emergency number. They're unable to locate our area, so I said they're being ridiculous. They're telling me we're somewhere across the Maharashtra border, near Gujarat... What rubbish, no?"

"Give me your phone." Abhay's face was unreadable.

"Uhh.. I mentioned the details. It's alright, Abhay. I think they're getting someone else to help."

"Your phone. Now." Abhay's tone left no room for argument.

Daksh sensed Kavya's phone was about to be taken. Kavya reluctantly handed it over.

Abhay answered, his tone firm. "Hello?"

"Hi.. Who's this?", a voice replied.

"I'm Kavya's husband, Abhay. You were talking to her earlier."

Abhay's gaze never left Kavya's face as he spoke. He ended the call, then checked Kavya's recent contacts. He had spoken to Officer Gupta and seen the unknown number. Kavya let out a sigh of relief.

"Abhay, please save Officer Gupta's number for me?" Kavya requested. Abhay nodded, his eyes still fixed on Kavya.

Kavya attempted to distract Abhay, asking, "Is the puncture fixed?"

Guru emerged from behind, wiping the wet mud from his hands. "There was no puncture, Tai. Only some damaged wires."

"What? How's that possible? We saw the tyre punctured ourselves!" Kavya was in disbelief.

"Yeah, I know, Kavya, but Guru's right. We checked all the tyres multiple times. Only twisted wires." Abhay chimed in.

"That's weird.. How?" She touched her forehead, confused,trying to process the information.

Guru's gaze drifted upward, his voice taking on a mystical tone. "I told you, didn't I? The forest and its secrets. The hares were the mystical creatures that brought you here, to trap you. It's all a conspiracy of the spirits of the forest.. It's the Chakwa..."

"I don't believe that, Guru. But I do agree it's all strange. Maybe someone fixed the tyre while we were away?" Abhay said, offering a logical reason.

"Maybe someone lives nearby? Some isolated habitation?" Kavya suggested.

As Kavya and Abhay exchanged skeptical glances, Guru began to chant a devotional mantra, his closed in reverence. "It's for protection. We villagers don't wish to upset the spirits of the forest."

As they prepared to leave, Abhay pulled out his wallet and handed some cash to Guru. "Anyway, thank you so much, Guru. Please, take this."

Guru hesitated, "Arey Dada, there wasn't much work needed to be done.." But Kavya insisted, "No, Guru, please have it. You've really been of great help. We'd be totally lost if it weren't for you."

Guru finally accepted the cash, placing it in a container. "It's getting dark. It's not advisable to stay here once it's dark."

Abhay nodded, "Yes, okay. We'll follow you on our way out. Is that alright?" Guru agreed, "Yes, sure, Dada. Just ensure to keep your windows shut and don't stop your car in between."

As they sat in their car, Abhay pulled out his spare phone. "We can use this phone, just in case, to contact Officer Gupta."

"Did you always have a spare phone in the car, Abhay?" Kavya raised an eyebrow.

"Not really, why?" Abhay replied.

Kavya shrugged. "Just...asking."

As they followed Guru out of the forest, they noticed the roads leading to the highway, the traffic lights, local shops buzzing with people, the children playing around. The contrast between the eerie forest and the bustling town was striking.

Guru stopped his truck on the side of the road, and Abhay and Kavya followed suit. "Dada, keep straight until you reach a crossroad. Take a right and you'll reach Khandi."

CHAPTER SEVENTEEN

CIRCLES... ON LOOP

Abhay thanked Guru again, and Kavya offered him some fruits for his journey back home. Guru bid them farewell, and they parted ways. As they drove away, Kavya called Officer Gupta to inform her that they'd finally found their way. Officer Gupta asked Kavya to keep her updated. Kavya then texted Daksh to let him know she was safe. Daksh was relieved to hear from her.

As they drove, Abhay suggested, "I'll check with the hotel reception if they still have our room reserved."

Kavya hesitated, "Abhay, I... I don't wish to go."

Abhay turned concerned, "I understand. The day was rough. Do you want to go home instead?"

Kavya shook her head, "No, not even home. I wish to go nowhere...with you."

"What do you mean? Where will you spend your night then?"

"I don't know. Haven't thought about it." Kavya shrugged.

Abhay narrowed his eyes, "Oh, really?? I thought Daksh made arrangements..like he did with Officer Gupta."

Kavya's smile hinted that she knew Abhay would deflect the conversation.

"So, Daksh, huh? It was Daksh on the call.. Kavya, he's been here just for a couple of months. You really are that gullible to believe a guy who once liked you and still does, possibly, to tell you 100% truth about your own husband?" Abhay's tone was accusatory.

"Abhay, I know everything." Kavya said calmly. "Abhay, you're right. Daksh has been here only for a couple of months. But what about someone who's been here all along in your life? Before me, before Riya... Maybe even before Daksh. And maybe that someone doesn't want anybody else before them?"

Abhay's honking became more aggressive, his patience wearing thin.

"I remember you said once your heart belongs here, Abhay. Just as it belonged in Canada once, then Bangalore. I now know the reason." Kavya said, her voice steady.

Abhay's defense rose, "Kavya, I swear Riya is out of the equation. I've moved on, and so has she. Just because she's moved here now----"

Kavya's expression was unyielding, "The custom-made cufflinks I gifted you.. You lied to me. You weren't in Delhi, were you?"

"I never lied to you. I don't have any reason to!"

"You sure didn't go to your colleague's funeral. That colleague had passed away days ago, with his funeral days ago when you left. The family doesn't even remember you visiting them."

Abhay's anger boiled over, "Why are you bringing all this now? Are you spying on me?"

"Because it's still not buried yet. Abhay, it all comes to the surface time and again. You try to bury it, but it just doesn't. I'm not spying on you, Abhay.. You're the one to talk? You've cloned my phone, haven't you?"

Abhay's expression turned sheepish, his eyes avoiding Kavya's. He touched his arm, revealing his tattoo.

"Your tattoo.. It was never Riya Hari.. The 'RH'... It was always Ravi Harne... He was the one who couldn't afford to move to Canada because of some paperwork, he was the one who decided to move to Bangalore instead. He was the one who texted Daksh the invite, using your spare phone, to make you and others believe that Daksh and I are together, so that I wouldn't know about you two.. or the fight in school. Ravi was jealous of you having feelings for Daksh, Ravi was the one who wants me out of your life... And maybe you do, too..."

The air was thick with tension as Kavya's words hung in the air. Abhay's face turned ashen, his eyes frozen on Kavya's. The silence that followed was deafening, a silence that pierced the soul. "What rubbish, Kavya?, always making up stories..."

As the car stereo played softly in the background, Abhay asked Kavya, "So what do you want now?"

Kavya gazed out the window, her eyes fixed on the fruit vendor in the distance. Abhay followed her gaze, and they both watched the as the fruit vendor misled another couple, guiding them in the wrong direction. Kavya's hand instinctively reached for the window handle, but Abhay's stern voice stopped her. "Don't open the window. Keep it shut." His tone firm, a warning underlying just as earlier.

As they drove on, Abhay took a sharp right turn at the crossroads.The evening sky had already surrendered to the darkness, with the sun dipping below the horizon. The flickering road lamps illuminated the isolated road ahead. The trees, like sentinels stood guard, their branches swaying ominously in the gentle breeze. As Abhay accelerated, the car devoured the distance, its tyres humming a monotonous tone. Suddenly, a hare darted across their path, its large luminous eyes gleaming in he fading light. The car's stereo now seamlessly transitioning to a melody that echoed the couple's predicament. Circles, Post Malone, playing in the background. "It's happening.... Again!" Kavya exclaimed.

Seasons change and our love went cold
Feed the flame 'cause we can't let it go
Run away, but we're running in circles
Run away, run away...

As the music played on, a half eaten apple fell from the glove box. The car hurtled forward, the hare's fleeting appearance. A harbinger of the couple's fate. Abhay tried to turn the steering wheel, attempting to avoid following the hare's direction. However, he was unable to.

"I don't know what's happening.." Panic creeping into his voice.

"Abhay, no.. Not again.. We shouldn't follow the hare," Kavya warned with desperation.

"The car's moving on its own and I have no control," Abhay shouted with fear.

The reality of their situation sank in, as they exchanged a knowing glance. They had ended up in Chakwa, a labyrinth from which there was no escape. The darkness of the forest seemed to seep into the car, enveloping them in an impenetrable shroud.

The song continued to play in the background, its lyrics echoing the Chakwa myth. The music faded into the distance.

Let go
I got a feeling that it's time to let go

I say so
I knew that this was doomed from the get-go
Maybe you don't understand what I'm going through
It's only me
What you got to lose?
Make up your mind, tell me
What are you gonna do?
It's only me
Let it go
Seasons change and our love went cold
Feed the flame 'cause we can't let it go
Run away, but we're running in circles
Run away, run away
I dare you to do something
I'm waiting on you again
So I don't take the blame
Run away, but we're running in circles
Run away, run away, run away...